Eclipse

ECLIPSE

KRISTINE L. FRANKLIN

CANDLEWICK PRESS
CAMBRIDGE, MASSACHUSETTS

First edition 1995

Library of Congress Cataloging-in-Publication Data

Franklin, Kristine L.
Eclipse / Kristine L. Franklin. — 1st U.S. ed.
Summary: When Trina's father falls into a severe depression
after losing his job and her mother becomes pregnant at
forty-eight, Trina faces a difficult summer even with the
help of her good friend Miranda.
ISBN 1-56402-544-6
[1. Mental illness — Fiction. 2. Pregnancy — Fiction. 3. Family
problems — Fiction. 4. Suicide — Fiction. 5. Friendship — Fiction.]
I. Title.
PZ7.F859224Wh   1995
[Fic] — dc20   94-14831

2 4 6 8 10 9 7 5 3 1

Printed in the United States

Candlewick Press
2067 Massachusetts Avenue
Cambridge, Massachusetts 02140

JFIC
FRA

For Lucy and Linda

MIRANDA said Mrs. Renchek looks like a pelican, but I didn't believe it until now. Her nose looks just like a beak! She's writing in a big notebook, probably putting little pronunciation marks around my last name so she'll get it right next time. "Katherine Jean Stenkawsky. Sten-COW-ski." She had me say my last name twice, the second time real slow, but that's nothing new. That's when I told her to call me Trina.

Grandma Stenkawsky could never pronounce *Kathy,* so right after I was born she started calling me Katerina. Pretty soon I was just Trina and it stuck. The only people who call me Kathy anymore are teachers on the first day of school. I'm used to it by now.

Every time Mrs. Renchek turns her head the skin of her neck flops around. I can almost imagine it full of fish, all stretched out and bulging and quivery. Mrs. Pelican.

It's hard to concentrate on this assignment. What kind of teacher gives you an assignment on the first day of school anyhow? *Gulp.* Looks like she just swallowed a fish. *Gulp.* Two fish. Miranda says she's nice even if she looks funny.

"Detailed and descriptive." That's what she said. About what we did last summer. My hands feel sweaty. And I've got that feeling in my stomach, like there's this big frog jumping around, trying to get out. If I had any fingernails left, I'd be eating them right now. After what I've been through in the last few days there isn't much to chew.

I'm always this nervous on the first day of school.

No, that's not really true.

It's because I don't want to write this paper. Too much happened last summer. There's no way to write it all down. Not in a million years. But I'd better write something, or she'll think I'm one of those kids who got all the way to seventh grade without knowing a thing. O.K., here goes.

What I Did Last Summer

by Trina Stenkawsky   English Rm. 5

Last summer I rode my horse a lot. His name is Chico and he's a gelding, not a stallion. That means he can't have children. My friend Miranda Evancich and I made a fort down in the gulch on the other side of the train tracks. Whenever we go there we race. Miranda's horse is named Tonka. Chico and Tonka have matching bridles. They were a present from Miranda's mom.

Chico is faster than Tonka, but Miranda keeps saying that Tonka should beat Chico because his legs are longer. Once I hit my knee really bad against a tree when we were racing, but it was only a bruise.

Miranda has this dog named Goofy. Goofy is an Airedale terrier, and if she doesn't get enough exercise, she jumps on everyone. All last summer Miranda brought Goofy on our rides. Afterward we would spend about an hour pulling burrs and stickers out of her fur. Once when Miranda was mad at me, she said my hair was just like Goofy's. Boring, brown, and fuzzy. At least my hair isn't carrot orange like hers.

Last summer I helped my mom with day care when my dad was in the hospital. He was sick. Mom paid me five dollars a week to help. I made lunch and Kool-Aid and watched the kids from nine to eleven in the morning so Mom could go to see a friend. There were four kids.

Wayne is five and he cries and fusses a lot. I call him Whine but not in front of his mom. Marissa is Wayne's little sister and she is two. She gets lots of ear infections and takes pink medicine, which she spits out. It's a pretty color, the medicine, I mean, but I don't like it all over my clothes.

Glendon is three years old. He has the biggest eyes, black like coal, my mom says. Glendon's mom had a baby last spring. The baby's name is Trinidad. It means Trinity in Spanish. Trinity is the Father, Son, and Holy Ghost. Trinidad started coming to day care right after school was out. He is the color of caramel (my favorite candy) and is fat and soft. He smiles a lot.

I don't miss the day-care kids, except for Trinidad and maybe Glendon a little, because I like how he said my name Tweena. My mom had a baby two weeks ago. So she can't do day care for a while. Our baby is still at the hospital. My dad is at a hospital too, but it's a different one. Before he went to the hospital, we watched an eclipse of the moon. It's pretty quiet at our house right now.

THE END

I hope Mrs. Pelican likes my paper. It's all true. The part about Marissa's medicine is detailed and descriptive. There's a lot more than what I wrote down, though. Some of it isn't too great. Some of it I'm trying hard not to think about, like Dad in the hospital, but no matter what I do, no matter what I think about or try to imagine, it's all still there, like a video playing over and over again. I wish there was a way to erase all the awful parts.

My summer really started in April, even though April is still in the spring. That's the day I found out the big news that changed everything. The reason I remember that day so well is because it was the day our cow Priscilla had her calf.

It was the Thursday before Easter, and I remember Mom saying how we never go to church anymore and what kind of Catholics are we anyway and we should at least go for Easter. She was changing Marissa's diaper on the bathroom floor, and Dad laughed and said church was the biggest waste of a Sunday morning he could think of and why should we start going again after all this time.

Marissa's diaper stank up the whole house, so I went outside to see Chico and mostly to escape the smell. Chico smells great, kind of a dried horse sweat and dust smell. It beats poopy diaper smell any day. But when I got to the barn, he was all jumpy and nervous and didn't want to eat his oats. Sometimes horses act up like that, so I smacked Chico on the rear and went to look for the shovel just outside his stall. That's how I found out the reason for Chico's mood. Outside the corral, on the other side of the fence where the grass grows, Priscilla was stretched out on her side and panting hard.

I left the shovel leaning against Chico's stall and ran into the house. "Dad! Mom!" I called. "Priscilla is having her calf!"

I'D been looking forward to this day ever since the guy from the artificial insemination place came last year. Dad doesn't use bulls. They're too dangerous. So the AI man comes and does the job with a long plastic glove. Last year I watched and asked questions. It was gross and interesting at the same time. Priscilla didn't seem to mind, and after a few weeks when she didn't go into heat again, we knew it had taken. I'd watched and kept track of her pregnancy ever since.

Priscilla's calf was going to be a Hereford, or half Hereford, half Jersey, because Priscilla's a Jersey. It wasn't due for another couple of weeks, or Dad would have locked Priscilla in the barn. He didn't look too happy when I told him.

I ran back outside, climbed over the fence, and tiptoed up to Priscilla's head. I didn't want to startle her. Her tongue was hanging out, and she was panting the way Goofy does after she chases a cat. I squatted down and scratched between her ears.

Priscilla is pretty old for a cow. Mom and Dad bought her three years before I was born. I'm twelve, so that makes her at least fifteen or sixteen. She gives milk that is so creamy it's like drinking a milk shake. Dad says he doesn't believe that good fresh cream could be bad for anyone, because Grandpa lived to be eighty-six and he always drank Jersey milk. Dad doesn't believe in fat and cholesterol. He's too skinny. I'm skinny too, just like Dad, and I'm going to be tall, like he is. Mom says you can tell by how big my feet are.

Dad's parents were dairy farmers in Poland before World War II. Dad says Grandpa always said a man with a cow is a rich man, and Dad believes it because even though we live in the city we have Priscilla. We aren't rich, though, so I'm not sure why Grandpa always said that. Before Priscilla it was Louise. Mom showed me a picture. Louise was a Jersey too.

Grandpa and Grandma bought our house when they first came to America. We got it after Grandma died. I was too little to remember moving. When Grandpa first came here it was the country. We have three acres, all fenced. The Abrigos next door have one. They're really nice, sort of like grandparents.

All along the train tracks in this part of town people still have some land. We all have barns too, left over from a long time ago. The Abrigos use theirs for a garage. The city has grown all around since Grandma and Grandpa were here, but we still have pasture, and so do our neighbors.

Only Miranda and I have horses. Only Dad has a cow. Dad trades all the apples and pears from two of our trees for the alfalfa that Mr. Abrigo grows on his acre. Mrs. Abrigo makes millions of gallons of applesauce and canned pears, and Chico and Priscilla get dinner in the winter. We couldn't afford alfalfa *and* oats without trading, so it's the only way I can have Chico. I guess in a way that makes me rich. A lot of girls would give anything to have a horse.

Priscilla has a calf every year. Dad fattens it up on grass and oats, and then in the fall he sells it. He says if we had more land he'd raise a dozen and we'd have more money, but we have only the three acres inside city limits, so we can't have a real farm.

By the time Mom and Dad came to see Priscilla, she was groaning. Mom made the day-care kids stay behind the fence and told me to go watch them to make sure they didn't try to crawl under. I climbed back over the fence and told Wayne to take the kids to the sandbox. He started whining about wanting to watch, but I told him to do it now or no Mister Rogers for a week. They went to the sandbox without a word.

Priscilla was rolling her eyes and slobber was hanging from her mouth. She had a terrified look in her eyes. Dad stood over her with his hands stuffed deep into his pockets. I couldn't tell by looking at his face if he was mad or just worried. The look is the same either way. He hates it when we wake him up from a nap, but he wasn't napping when I went in, so I wasn't sure what there was to be mad about. I wondered if something was wrong with Priscilla, but I didn't ask. It's best not to bother my dad when he has that look.

Last year Dad broke his back. He was in the hospital for a super long time, and when he got out, he couldn't go back to work. His back still hurts. That's why he sort of slumps. It's bad posture but he can't help it. He had on his blue overalls and his oldest barn boots, the ones that are cut off short so he can get them on in a hurry without bending over. Dad has wild gray hair that sticks straight up unless he glues it down with hair goop. He ran a big hand through his hair and it looked even wilder.

Mom was squatting on the ground behind Priscilla, one hand on Priscilla's belly. "It's probably breech," said Dad. "Go on and feel for the feet." Mom moved around to Priscilla's backside, lifted her tail, pushed her shirtsleeve all the way to her shoulder, and slowly put her hand into Priscilla. I swallowed hard. Vets and AI guys do it all the time, but this was my mom, and it makes a difference. She's little and pudgy, and her arms aren't that long. Could a person's arm get stuck in there? It was a dumb thought, but I thought it anyway.

There was some watery stuff and a little blood, and poor Priscilla just moaned and groaned. Her huge belly humped up like a mountain every time she grunted. Now Mom's arm was in up to the elbow. Priscilla was swallowing her.

"Feel anything yet?" shouted Dad, even though Mom was right there. He wiped his hands on his overalls. Ever since Dad hurt his back, he's had to be careful. I could tell he wanted to be feeling for Priscilla's calf himself. His arms were so much longer. This time only Mom could help Priscilla. Her arm was in almost to her shoulder.

"I'm touching the feet, Mitch," said Mom. "They're turned somehow." She took a deep breath. "I'll try to straighten them."

Priscilla held her breath and pushed. "*Ow!*" cried Mom, and I stuck my finger in my mouth and bit hard on a piece of fingernail. "She's really working to get this guy out." Mom felt around inside Priscilla. It made a squishy sound that grossed me out.

Mom had a concentrated look on her face, the same look she has when she figures out how much money is in the bank. Dad paced back and forth in that limping way of his. He talked and talked, which is weird for him.

"Don't move too fast," he yelled. "Get hold of the feet, get a good hold. Have you got it yet? I can't lose both of them."

All of a sudden I realized that if the calf didn't come out soon, Priscilla might die! No wonder Dad was acting so nervous. My heart started to pump in my ears, and I held my breath every time Priscilla did. Her moaning sounded so pitiful, so horrible. I couldn't stop watching.

"I can't straighten them," said Mom. "There's something wrong."

"Then grab hold and pull with every contraction," said Dad, "but not hard. Steady. Pull, Anita. Come *on*, Priscilla."

It seemed like three hours but was only a few minutes before I saw that Mom's arm was on its way out. It was so bloody I felt like barfing, but I swallowed it down and kept watching. When it got down to her hand I could see she was hanging on to something hard covered by a slimy, bluish white transparent skin. With one more big push the calf was born, slipping out onto the grass with a gush of water and blood. Mom didn't even wipe her hand off. She was already at Priscilla's head, trying to get her to stand up.

"Come on, Prissy," said Mom. "Get up." She pulled on Priscilla's halter, and Dad pushed a little from behind with his foot until she stood up on shaky legs and turned around to see her baby. The calf hadn't moved yet. Dad leaned down and peeled the filmy stuff off from around its nose. I heard a little sputter, but it was hard to see from the fence because now Priscilla was trying to lick her calf while Dad and Mom stood around making sure everything was O.K.

They didn't say anything, just looked down.

"Is it a boy or a girl?" I called from the fence.

"Quiet, Trina," said Mom. Her voice was tired and her arm was still bloody. It hung by her side like something out of a horror movie. I wished she'd wipe it off.

Now the calf was struggling and kicking its legs. I knew it should try to stand right away, but it just lay there kicking.

"I'll take care of it," said Dad to Mom. His shoulders slumped more than ever and when he sighed his whole body shook. Mom nodded.

"What a shame," she said, shaking her head. She took Priscilla by the halter and pulled her away from the calf and into the barn. Big strings of gooey afterbirth hung out of her. She kept trying to look at her baby.

I looked over at the sandbox. Glendon and Marissa were fighting over a headless GI Joe. Wayne was digging a hole with a spoon. I jumped over the fence and went to look at the calf. That's when I saw what was wrong. The calf's front legs were turned under in a funny way.

Dad patted the calf on the head. Its white face was wet and its big blue eyes looked up at us. It had white eyelashes, maybe two inches long, and its shiny nose was the same pink as those tiny roses ladies at church get when they have a baby girl. *Maaaa*, said the calf and kicked around. Its legs were really crooked.

"Are you going to call the vet?" I asked.

"Vet can't do a thing for a deformed calf," said Dad. He pulled up a bunch of buttercups that were smashed into the grass next to the calf and tossed them toward the fence. "I'll have to take care of it myself."

He stood up painfully and brushed his hands on his overalls. "Get inside, Trina," said Dad, "and the little kids too." He looked over toward the barn. Mom had locked Priscilla in her stall, and now the old cow started to cry. *Mooooo*, she called. *Moooooo!* It was a desperate sound, like wind howling across the chimney or trees creaking in a storm. It made me shiver, but not because I was cold. "Now get!" yelled Dad, and his voice made me jump.

"But the poor calf—" I started to say, but he cut me off with a smack on the shoulder. I grabbed my shoulder and backed away.

"Forget about this calf!" he shouted. His face was red and his eyes were bulging, and I think I even saw the beginnings of tears, though he wasn't exactly acting sad. He stomped past me and headed for the house.

I rubbed my shoulder all the way to the fence, my own tears stinging in my eyes. Dad doesn't smack me much, but when he does I hate it. I didn't look back at the little calf. Dad was going to take care of it. Deep inside I knew what that meant, though it was too horrible to actually think the words.

I concentrated on climbing over the fence. Then I

dragged the kids out of the sandbox. Marissa had dumped sand into her diaper, and Wayne's nose was running green slime mixed with dirt. Glendon was crying because Wayne told him the headless GI Joe was going to get him. I told them they could watch cartoons. That got their attention.

Just then Dad came limping out of the house. I didn't even have to look to know what the dark metal thing was that he had in his hand. I've never touched it. He keeps it locked away in a cabinet, and I'd be in major trouble if I even went near it. I knew he had it, but I didn't want to see, hear, or think about it.

I shook the sand out of Marissa's diaper. It was still dry, so the sand came out without sticking. I took the kids inside, turned on the TV extra loud, and stared at the bright cartoon people.

Mom was in the bathroom cleaning up. Even with the TV on I could hear the shower. I heard the water turn off and the toilet seat go up with a bang. Then I heard my Mom throw up. I hurried to the door.

"Mom?" I said through the door. "Are you okay?" The toilet flushed and Mom answered in a weak voice.

"Okay." Then I heard her laugh a little. "Okay for a forty-eight-year-old pregnant lady," she said. The door opened, and she stood there in her robe smelling of Ivory soap and shampoo and of barf. A big smile stretched across her face and showed the wrinkles around her mouth and eyes, the ones she calls laugh lines. She was a little pale, and her eyes looked extra big and extra blue, but I could see the happiness in them. "You're going to be a sister."

A baby. Another kid. I wouldn't be an only child anymore.

Boom! We both heard it. Outside. Even with the TV turned up loud. Neither of us said a word.

A strand of gray hair flopped down into Mom's face, and she blew it away with a *poof.* I stared at her stomach, pretending I hadn't heard the shot.

"So what do you think?" Mom asked. She wasn't talking about the calf.

"Does Dad know?" I asked. Maybe she *was* a little fatter, but then she was pretty fat to start with.

"Of course." She patted my head like I was a one of the little day-care kids. I hate that. "The baby will be born in September. Dad's known for a while." Of course Dad would know, I thought. What a dumb question! The thought of my parents doing it was kind of gross. They're so *old!*

"How come you didn't tell me before?" I asked.

I added it up in my head. She was four months pregnant. I saw an ad in a magazine once for a test to know right away if you're pregnant. It bugged me that she'd waited so long.

"Well, because of my age, I guess. I didn't want you to get your hopes up, in case anything happened. A lot can go wrong with a pregnancy when the mother is forty-eight years old." *Kind of like when a cow is fifteen or sixteen,* I thought. "I've had a lot of miscarriages, Trina."

Oh yeah, that. It was the only time I'd seen Mom really bawl. She went to the hospital once when I was six. The neighbors' kid, Tony Abrigo, came to baby-sit and gave me bread-and-butter sandwiches for dinner. When she came home Mom said she'd had a baby growing inside but that God had taken it to heaven early and not to be sad. I remember her crying and crying, the tears dripping off her chin and nose when she said the part about not being sad, and I wanted to cry too, but I didn't. For a whole month after that I prayed for God to give us another baby, but nothing happened. I didn't say any prayers for a long time after that, not even "Now I Lay Me Down to Sleep."

Mom was going to have a baby.

"I didn't want you to be sad if anything happened," said Mom with a smile. "I didn't want you to worry."

"You still could have told me," I said, wishing she didn't protect me so much, like I was still a little kid.

"Are you happy about it?" asked Mom, her eyes looking around on my face for clues, but there weren't any clues, not yet. I was still in shock from the news. *A baby!* It was amazing news.

Just then Glendon fell off the couch, and I didn't have time to answer her question about being happy. His head hit the floor with a *klonk*, and Marissa started screaming because he'd knocked over her blocks, and Wayne the Whiner started whining that he couldn't see Mister Rogers. Mom went to fix up the kids, and I fixed myself a peanut butter sandwich. Dinner would be in an hour or so, but I was starving. I couldn't wait.

Are you happy about it? Mom's words echoed in my brain.

Priscilla mooed out in the barn. What was Dad doing now? Glendon sniffled in the other room. I heard Mom tear open a package of graham crackers and offer them to the kids. I took a big bite of my sandwich and slumped into a chair.

I was going to be a sister! Of course I was happy!

I never found out if the calf was a boy or a girl. No one said. Mom acted like nothing had happened. Dad started taking naps twice a day, and when he wasn't sleeping he had his stay-outa-my-way look on his face. I was afraid to ask him about the calf. I was afraid he might get mad. I looked out in the pasture for a little grave or something, anything, but Dad had taken care of it and that was that.

Priscilla stood in the barn for two days, mooing all the time, milk dripping from her huge, swollen udder. Dad milked her some, enough to get rid of the first yellow milk, which isn't any good for people to drink. When he milked her she seemed happier, at least for a couple of minutes. Then she would start to moo again, swaying in her stall and swishing her tail back and forth, back and forth, even though it was too early for flies.

When Dad finally let her out of the barn, she mooed all over the pasture, running between the trees and looking for her calf. After about a week she got tired of being sad, or maybe she just forgot about the calf, but she stopped mooing and went back to being a quiet, big-eyed old cow.

I think it must be nice to be a cow and forget sad things so fast. I wish I could do that too. Then maybe I wouldn't have a frog in my stomach all the time. Maybe I'd have long, gorgeous fingernails like Miranda's mom.

After Mom told me about the baby, she didn't talk about it again. Dad didn't act like he even knew. Isn't that kind of strange? I mean, don't families get all excited, pick names, and buy baby clothes? I wasn't sure how to feel or what to say or if it would be O.K. to ask questions. I think Dad was upset about losing the calf, but I couldn't be sure because no one said. Dad counted on the calf money every year, and now it was gone. That's enough to put anyone in a bad mood.

I rode Chico whenever I wasn't at school or helping Mom. It helped me not think about the calf, about Mom and the baby, and how Mom and Dad weren't talking much. Miranda and I rode down to the gulch and made a camp between two huge sticker bushes. We went there almost every day. That's where we were when I told Miranda about the baby.

It was after school on a Wednesday, and neither of us had to be back until five-thirty, so we were lying around on the grass in our camp. Goofy was barking at a squirrel in a tree. Chico and Tonka were tied to another tree, and I could hear Chico stomping. He doesn't like it if another horse gets too close. Once he kicked Tonka right in the nose and made a nick that bled. Miranda got mad, but I asked her how would she like a horse's nose in her behind, and that made her laugh and then she wasn't mad anymore. Miranda doesn't stay mad for long.

Miranda had two cans of Coke and I had a can of Pringles, the onion kind. We were munching and drinking, and I was thinking that the smell of new grass is just about the best smell of springtime next to cherry blossoms when Miranda said she wished Tonka was a mare so she could have a foal.

"Wouldn't a baby palomino be cute?" she said, and then she burped out loud and we both cracked up. Miranda has that Pippi Longstocking look, all freckly and flat-chested with a naughty sparkle in her eye, but her mom is really prissy and bugs her to keep clean and be a lady. She even got Miranda an English saddle when she asked for a Western! So Miranda never uses a saddle. Neither do I, but that's because I don't have one. And Miranda is never supposed to burp out loud. That's why it's extra funny.

"Guess what?" I said. "My mom's having a baby in September."

Miranda's brown eyes got huge. "You've got to be joking," she said, and the way she said it sounded just like a grown-up.

"Why would I joke about that?" I felt the smile slide off my face.

"But your mom is so *old*," said Miranda. "What if it comes out retarded?"

"Forty-eight isn't *that* old," I said.

"My grandma is only fifty-two," said Miranda.

"What do you mean, retarded?" I sat up and gulped down the rest of my Coke. The can of Pringles was only half empty, but I didn't feel like eating anymore.

"My mom has this big health book," said Miranda. She stuffed a stack of chips in her mouth. "It says old women should never have babies, because they might turn out retarded. It's a gene thing." A couple of potato chip crumbs fell out of her mouth.

"Shut up, Miranda," I said. I got up and brushed off my jeans. "I wish I hadn't told you."

"I'm sorry," she said. "It just came out." Miranda hardly ever thinks before she says something. It's one of those things her mom constantly nags her about, that and burping. Miranda hung her arm around my neck and grinned. "I cross my heart I won't say anything more about your mom being old and babies that come out you-know-what." We walked to the horses with Miranda hanging on me, but I didn't feel like talking. For a minute I wished I would never see Miranda again. *Retarded!* I felt grouchy and confused, and the Pringles and Coke gave me onion burps that made me feel sick.

My mom *was* old. Old enough to be a grandma! What if something was wrong with the baby? What if I had a retard for a brother or sister? Thinking about it gave me a yucky feeling inside, kind of scared and mad at the same time. If old women shouldn't have babies, why had Mom let herself get pregnant?

We raced Chico and Tonka to Miranda's house, and while the air was whooshing past my cheeks I forgot about what she'd said. Then when we came galloping around the last corner, I saw Miranda's mom standing on the front porch of their house paying the newspaper girl. Mrs. Evancich is so pretty and young everyone would be happy if she had a baby. I waved good-bye to Miranda and her mom and turned

Chico down the alley toward home. Goofy tried to follow me until I yelled at her to go home. When I got to my house I was thinking about old moms again.

I came in the back door just in time to hear Glendon's dad say good-bye from the other room, and the front door shut. Wayne and Marissa's mom never came until after dinner. My jeans were sweaty and full of hair from riding bareback, so I kicked off my shoes, pulled off my jeans, and threw them in the laundry pile by the washing machine. I grabbed a pair of clean shorts out of the dryer, slipped into them, and went inside to find something to eat.

"I'm back," I called to anyone who cared. Marissa was asking for Cheerios.

"Hi, Trina," called Mom. "Have a good ride?"

"Yeah," I mumbled, and stuck my head in the fridge. It was pretty empty. I shut the door and wandered into the living room. Mom was sitting in the rocking chair with Marissa in her lap. Marissa had a little cup of Cheerios. In her other arm she clutched an old yellow blanket with faded pink spots from the earache medicine. Mom rocked her back and forth, humming the "Sesame Street" song. Marissa loves that show. Wayne was sucking his thumb. Dad was asleep on the couch. I picked my way over trucks, two Barbie dolls, and the Etch-a-Sketch and sat on the stool next to Mom. I was trying to get brave enough to tell her what Miranda said.

"Guess what?" asked Mom. She petted Marissa's straggly yellow curls with one hand. "Glendon's mom had her baby. It's a boy. Nine pounds!"

"Is he all okay?" I asked. "Like a normal baby?" Glendon's mom is a lawyer. She's older too. And his dad has gray hair.

"Of course, Trina," said Mom. "What a funny question." Maybe it was a funny question to her, but to me it was important.

"What's his name?" I asked.

"The baby's name is Trinidad," said Mom. "Isn't that a cute name?"

"It's an island, Mom. Are you sure that's what he said?"

"Glendon's dad says it's Spanish for the Trinity."

"You mean Father, Son, and Holy Ghost? Like in God?" Mom nodded.

"Why would they give him a name like Father, Son, and Holy Ghost?" I asked.

Mom laughed. "I guess they're better Catholics than we are," she said.

We used to go to church before Dad lost his job. Miranda and I always sat together. Just about every week one of us would have a giggling attack. Something funny would always happen, like Father Tom would spit while he was talking or one of the altar boys would pick his nose or Mr. Abrigo would fart when he tried to kneel down for the prayer, and then the silent laughing spasms would start. We'd shake and sputter, and our faces would turn red until one of our moms would do something. My mom always yanked ears. Mrs. Evancich poked with those long nails of hers. Sometimes it was so bad I could hardly look at Miranda without having to bite my cheek. I missed church a lot.

Now Mom, Marissa, and Wayne were watching Big Bird roller-skate down Sesame Street. Marissa knocked the cup of Cheerios to the floor and started to scream. Wayne shouted, "Shut up, Missy!" and Dad woke up.

"Anita, can't you keep those kids quiet?" he yelled. He struggled to sit up. He swung his long legs around to the front of the couch, stood up, hiked up his pants, which were hanging pretty low, and limped out to the kitchen. I heard the door to the back porch open and slam shut, and then the garden tools rattled on their hooks. Mom and I looked at each other, but we didn't say anything.

Dad didn't come back until after dinner.

We had chili, the kind without meat, and lots of milk. Wayne and Marissa wouldn't eat the chili, so Mom fixed them peanut butter on crackers. I ate three bowls of chili and drank two glasses of Priscilla's thick milk. I wondered what Dad was doing. Probably planting something. He does that when he's upset.

Wayne and Marissa went home at seven. Mom and I did the dishes. I kept looking at her sideways, looking at her belly, where my brother or sister was growing, wondering what it or he or she would be like, wondering if my mom was worried about being too old. Mom's face was pale and puffy-looking around the eyes, and her gray hair hung around her face like string. Her shoulders drooped and one corner of her mouth twitched. She didn't talk to me at all, like I wasn't even there. She dried the dishes slowly, wiping each one like it was Queen Elizabeth's china instead of plain old white Corningware. I kept wanting to ask her, I mean about being old and babies that come out retarded, but every time I looked at her tired face I chickened out.

After we finished the dishes I went upstairs to practice my lines for the Cultural Arts Week puppet play. The theme was Land of the Maya, and Miranda and I had written a play about the Mayan Indians' belief of how monkeys were created. It was from a book I'd read. Other kids were doing speeches and art projects, but Miranda said we'd have to do something different if we wanted to win the competition. None of the other kids were doing puppets.

I was feeling kind of nervous about the whole thing. Even though no one would be able to see us, we would still be in front of people. I read my lines out loud, thinking through the moves we had practiced. I giggled to myself at the funny parts. Miranda had written those. I was almost at the end of the play when Dad came in. I heard the back door slam. Mom was still downstairs, picking up the mess from the day, getting ready for the the next day's mess. Dad started to mutter low and fast, the way he does when he's super mad. It was a scary sound, almost crazy. He's always had a bad temper, but ever since he lost his job he's been yelling a lot more.

I wanted to bury my head under my pillow and hum "Happy Birthday" really loud, like I did when I was little. It always made the fights go faster. I would count how many times I could hum "Happy Birthday" before the yelling was over, humming so loud it hurt inside my head. And the next morning everything would be fine. The day-care kids would come early, Dad would go off to work, and Mom would smile and ask if I'd had sweet dreams. That was just regular Mom and Dad–type fighting. This was different somehow.

I didn't hum. I held my breath and listened.

"No!" yelled Dad. "I can't handle any more kids around here."

How weird. Dad always liked the day-care kids. He always said the more the merrier. Why would he be yelling at Mom about them now?

"A man oughta be done with babies when he's fifty-three years old!" he said. "It's too late for more. Too late!" Mom said something, but it was too quiet to hear.

"Don't talk to me about money!" shouted Dad. I heard his fist hit the kitchen table.

We almost never have enough money. The only money we get is Dad's disability and the money Mom earns from day care. As long as we have at least three kids in day care we can get by. Four is better. That's why Mom was so happy about Glendon's little brother. If we have four kids there is even a little extra money.

I didn't understand why Dad was making such a fuss about one more baby at day care, but it didn't sound like he wanted Trinidad around.

"I *told* you Anita," yelled Dad. "I told you no! No, no, no! No more kids, I said. How come you didn't listen to me? Huh? You never listen to me." I still couldn't hear what Mom was saying.

Wayne, Marissa, and Glendon. I thought about those three little kids and how quiet our house would be without them. Mom had been saying we needed one more kid. Trinidad would make four. Then there would be enough money. Dad could stop worrying. It would make up for the dead calf. And if Mom couldn't take Trinidad, Glendon's parents would change baby-sitters and we'd have even less money. We'd had Glendon since he was born. I showed him how to walk, letting him hold my fingers while he took little steps. Glendon's parents paid well, were nice, and always picked up on time. It would be stupid not to take Trinidad. Mom raised her voice. Now I could hear her words.

"Mitch, we've waited so long." Her voice was quavery and upset. "This is for you, for Trina, for all of us. It's the miracle we've prayed for."

"I don't believe in praying anymore," said Dad. "Not after losing my job like that."

"I just want you to be happy about it," said Mom. "Please try."

"I'm too old for this," wailed Dad, almost like he was going to cry! I'd never heard my Dad cry, never in my life. I listened even harder. "I didn't think it was possible," he said. "What if something goes wrong?"

Now I knew for sure that he was crying. It was an awful, sickening sound. My tall, strong Dad, who used to carry me on his shoulders and laugh at my pigtails that stuck straight out, was blubbering like a baby.

"What am I gonna do now?" Dad sobbed. "What am I gonna do now?"

"Just be a good father," said Mom. "As always."

It was like someone had punched me in the stomach.

All at once I realized that they weren't arguing about Glendon and Trinidad or any of the day-care kids. They were arguing about the baby, Mom's baby. The one that Miranda said old women shouldn't have because it might turn out wrong. Dad didn't want it. Dad didn't want my brother or sister. And he was crying about it!

I couldn't listen anymore. I buried my head under the pillow.

Happy birthday to you,
Happy birthday to you,
Happy birthday dear baby . . .

Then I cried until I fell asleep.

I woke up early the next morning because some robins were *pip-pip-pipping* right outside my window. I got dressed for school and went downstairs. When I got to the kitchen Mom was fixing Cheerios for the three kids. Someone was sitting in a poopy diaper. Dad wasn't around.

I poured myself a bowl of Cheerios and put two pieces of bread in the toaster. "Did you have sweet dreams?" asked Mom in a cheerful voice.

"Yeah." I lied.

"When's that puppet show you and Miranda have been working so hard on?" She cut a piece of bread into four triangles and put them on little plates. Maybe she couldn't smell the poop.

"Today," I said, buttering my toast. "All the performance things are today."

"What are the other kids doing?" She poured orange juice into a cup and stuck a lid on it, the kind with a spout for little kids.

"Oh, skits, speeches, stuff like that. Robin Frei wrote a song." My toast popped up. It was black around the edges.

"I'm sure you girls will do well," she said. Mom's voice was happy, but she had a little line between her eyes, and her shoulders drooped so much it made her belly stick out. She did look old. Old enough to be a plump little grandma. Too old to be a new mom. Marissa slapped Glendon. Glendon knocked Marissa's bread to the floor.

"I don't know," I said, talking loudly. "It's pretty hard to win. There's a lot of competition." Cultural Arts Week was a big deal at my school. There would be models, paintings, and stories, as well as all the performance entries. Juliana Drexler was even making ceramic copies of Mayan jewelry. Her mom is a potter.

I wanted to win more than anything. The grand prize was a free week at YMCA camp. Miranda was already planning how we would be bunk mates. Every time we talked about winning she'd start singing "Kumbaya." But after last night, how could I remember my lines? How can a girl get excited about the Land of the Maya or even YMCA camp when everything at home is turning out so rotten?

"Just do your very best," said Mom, pushing the two high chairs apart so Glendon and Marissa couldn't touch. "And don't be nervous."

"Miranda and I have been practicing," I said. Before we finished building the puppet theater we used the back of the Evancichs' couch. The first time we did it, the green paint on one of the puppets' heads wasn't dry. Mrs. Evancich had a total fit over the spot it made.

"I doubt if anyone has worked as hard as you two," said Mom. She wiped her hands and took a sip of her coffee. Then she sighed, stood up, and patted me on the arm. "Enjoy yourself, Trina Jean."

Mom didn't say anything about the fight, but there it was, hanging in the air between us. She calls me Trina Jean only at certain times, when she feels extra motherly or something. She knew I knew about last night. I could tell by her look, her sigh, and the way she patted my arm.

"Mom," I said.

"Yes?" She was smiling, but it was a tired smile. Did she know what I was going to say?

"I heard you guys last night." Mom nodded and looked out the window. "About the baby," I said. I waited for her to say something. The wall clock ticked. Marissa dropped her spoon.

"Dad's got a lot on his mind these days," said Mom. "He . . ." She bit her lip and didn't finish what she was going to say. She shook her head and smiled at me. "Don't worry about Dad, Trina," said Mom. "I can take care of that skinny old husband of mine."

"But he doesn't want the baby!" I couldn't believe I'd said it out loud. Mom's eyes got big. She put her hand on my cheek and shook her head.

"Of *course* he wants the baby," said Mom. "He was just upset. People say silly things when they're upset. Everything will be okay."

Right then I wanted to jump up and hug her, sit on her lap the way I used to, before I got long legs. I wanted to tell her that she was right, that everything would be O.K., but I'm twelve years old, too old for laps, and I was getting that choking feeling in my throat, which I hate. Mom was right. Dad was just upset. I say stupid things when I'm upset.

Doesn't everyone? What dad wouldn't want his own baby? *Unless it was messed up because the mom was too old.* I didn't say it, but I thought it. It was time to go to school.

"See you after school, Mom," I said. I grabbed my books and hurried out the door before she could see my lower lip twitching. "Have a nice day," I yelled from the driveway. She was standing in the doorway waving and smiling, but her eyes were the saddest I'd ever seen.

We had to work on our maps of Central America for the first hour of school. I'm not a good artist but I like maps. I tried hard not to think about moms and dads and retarded babies. I thought a lot about the puppet play, but not enough to get nervous. That would come later. I worked on Costa Rica and drew a coffee bush with little red berries right in the middle of the country.

Miranda and I gave each other looks across the room, and I almost cracked up when she made a face and made her hands talk to each other like puppets. She was thinking about it too.

Finally Mr. Durkovic said that anyone who had to get ready for the Cultural Arts Week competition could leave. Miranda jumped up and knocked over her chair with her gym bag. I grabbed the scripts out of my notebook. We hurried to the auditorium along with a group of boys from our class who were doing a skit. When we got there, other sixth-grade kids from other classes were filling in the front rows. Mrs. Lu, one of the sixth-grade teachers, stood in front with a clipboard.

"Each group has five minutes to set up," she said, "starting with the students from Mr. Russell's class, then mine, then Mr. Durkovic's. Make sure all of your props are behind the back curtain and ready to move out onstage when your turn is called." There were four skits, one dance thing, and our puppet play. We were after the skit kids. Miranda whispered the whole time, commenting on each group of kids and how they could never beat us. I nibbled my fingernails until it was our turn.

Our puppet theater was already backstage. Miranda's dad had brought it to school the week before. We unfolded the two sides and stood it up. Except for cutting the boards and attaching the hinges, Miranda and I had done everything, even the curtains and the sheet up above that held our surprise special effect. The front was painted with jungle trees, volcanoes, and clouds, with sky behind. I pulled the little curtains across and set up the special effects for the end of the play. My hands were sweaty and my stomach was churning. Miranda talked the whole time, but I didn't pay attention.

Miranda took the puppets out of her gym bag and laid them in a row behind the puppet theater. "Now all we have to do is scoot the whole thing to center stage and we'll be ready. Aren't you excited?" I nodded but didn't answer. My mouth felt dry.

We finished up, and the next group of kids came onstage to get ready. Miranda and I sat back in our seats. "Now I'll read the order of events," said Mrs. Lu, "so be ready to go when your turn comes." We were seventh. Then she looked at her watch. "At ten o'clock all the teachers will bring their classes in for the performances. Good luck to you all."

Miranda grabbed my arm and squeezed hard. "Oh, I can't wait!" she said. "I just can't stand waiting!" I slumped in my seat, opened my script, and read through my lines. I had a lot of lines. All the narration, in fact. Miranda had talked me into being the narrator. "You have such a melodic voice," she'd said. The pages were soon rumpled-looking from my sweaty hands. I thought about all those kids doing skits. I thought about the girls who were going to dance. That was pretty creative, dancing, I mean. Puppets were for little kids. This sick feeling sort of crept up toward my head from my stomach. Everyone would think puppets were stupid. Why didn't we do a skit, or paint quetzal birds or something? Why did I always let Miranda talk me into these things?

The program started with the principal, Ms. Linstrom, giving a boring speech about the many cultures of the Americas and how we were going to celebrate the Land of the Maya all week, blah-blah-blah. She talked about the prizes and the dance at the end of the week. I concentrated on my script.

The first kid who went gave a speech. She kept coughing and saying "um." It was something about how the Mayans built their temples. The next thing was Robin Frei. She had some tape-recorded music of herself playing the piano. She sang along and a lot of kids laughed, which is mean, but it was because Robin thinks she is such a great singer.

There were three skits in a row. The boys from our class were the funniest. They did a thing where they played the

Mayan ball game, the one with the balls that you hit with your hips and elbows. (They faked the ball, since they were onstage.) They fell down, ran around, swung their hips all over, and whacked each other with their butts. When they got to the end, where the loser-team guys get sacrificed to the gods, they popped bags of ketchup on their chests and pulled out pieces of meat for their hearts. Everyone was grossed out, but it was funny. I forgot about the puppet play long enough to crack up.

There was one more speech. My hands were sweaty. I could hardly swallow. Miranda kept grabbing me, and I didn't hear one word of that speech. All I could think of was our turn. I knew the speech was over because everyone clapped. It was our turn. We slipped out from our seats and went backstage. I had to pee so badly I could hardly stand it, but there was no time to go to the bathroom. This was *it*.

The lights on the stage were hot. My heart throbbed in my throat as I helped Miranda push our puppet stage out into the middle. Kids were talking and giggling. I took some deep breaths. Miranda got the microphone and brought it around behind the stage. "Testing, one-two-three," she said. The mike worked fine. I pulled two stools behind the stage and sat down. I opened my script and put it on my lap. Miranda set the mike carefully in the cardboard holder we'd made. It was right in front of my face. She put a puppet on her hand. I put one puppet on my hand. I swallowed. Everyone was quiet now. I swallowed again and started to read.

"The following story is taken from the Mayan book of mythology called *The Popul Vuh*." My voice sounded totally different through the microphone, not like me at all. For some reason it made me feel less nervous.

"*The Popul Vuh* tells how everything in the world was created by the gods. This story is called 'The Wooden People.'" I rolled my eyes. Miranda gave me the O.K. with her free hand. I took another deep breath and the play began.

"HEART of Heaven and Heart of Earth were gods," I narrated.

Miranda's puppet was Heart of Heaven, and mine was Heart of Earth. We'd copied their heads from pictures in the encyclopedia.

"Heart of Heaven ruled the sky. Heart of Earth ruled the world." We popped the puppets up and walked them across the stage. "Every day Heart of Heaven pushed the sun across the sky. Every day he blew the clouds into piles." I blew into the mike.

"Heart of Earth shook the world with her earthquakes." Miranda shook the puppet stage. "She cracked open canyons, and when she burped, well, it was a natural disaster." Miranda burped into the mike. Everyone laughed.

"Being deities, Heart of Heaven and Heart of Earth fought a lot." Puppets fighting.

MY PUPPET. Just look at my lovely new continent.

MIRANDA'S PUPPET. That ugly pile of rocks? *[More fighting]*.

NARRATOR *[Me]*. Life went on this way for zillions of years. Then one day, after a satisfying eruption

[Miranda burps again], Heart of Earth got an idea.

MY PUPPET. H.H., we should stop bickering and work together on a project.

MIRANDA'S PUPPET. What exactly did you have in mind?

MY PUPPET. Subjects. What we need are subjects, you know, creatures that fear and worship us. We could rule them.

NARRATOR. So together they created the birds and animals. Heart of Heaven and Heart of Earth were happy for about six million years.

MIRANDA'S PUPPET. Just listen to those subjects. The larks are larking, the jaguars jagging—

MY PUPPET. Jaguars howl.

MIRANDA'S PUPPET. Whatever. At least they worship us.

MY PUPPET *[Pouty voice].* Yes, but they aren't scared of us. And they never bring us sacrifices. All my god friends get sacrifices.

MIRANDA'S PUPPET. Gripe, gripe, gripe. *[Puppet theater shakes].* Okay, okay. Knock off all the quaking. We'll make new subjects.

NARRATOR. So Heart of Heaven and Heart of Earth set out to make some better, more scared subjects. At first they argued about what material to make the new subjects out of.

MY PUPPET. I say clay.

MIRANDA'S PUPPET. I say wood. It's more practical.

MY PUPPET *[Pouty voice].* You have no sense of art.

NARRATOR. In the end they agreed to use wood *[Miranda*

put on one of the wooden people puppets]. Finally the work was finished. *[I put on the other wooden person. Now there were two.]*

MIRANDA'S PUPPET. Let's call these creatures quatlquetlbotlmetl.

MY PUPPET. How about people? It's a lot simpler.

MIRANDA'S PUPPET. People. I like it. *[People puppets walk around].*

NARRATOR. The wooden people looked a lot like you and me. They were a jolly, happy race, enough to make any god proud. There was only one problem. The wooden people weren't afraid of anything.

When they got too close to the edge of a cliff, they fell over *[Puppets fall]*. When it rained, they stood outside until their arms warped *[Sound of wind]*. Heart of Heaven and Heart of Earth spent all their time rescuing the wooden people. Then, one day . . .

MIRANDA'S PUPPET. What's that smell? *[Sound of sniffing]*.

MY PUPPET. Oh, just a little wood smoke.

MIRANDA'S PUPPET *[Mad voice]*. You gave them *fire?* Those idiots will burn up the whole world!

MY PUPPET *[Whine]*. I'm tired of rescuing them.

MIRANDA'S PUPPET. You had to have better subjects! You had to have sacrifices!

MY PUPPET. It wasn't me who forgot to give them brains.

NARRATOR. Lightning bolts zigzagged across the sky. The rain poured down *[Scary sounds in mike]*.

MY PUPPET. Be careful! You'll drown them.

MIRANDA'S PUPPET. It *would* solve our little problem.

NARRATOR *[Thunder sound in mike]*. The water began to rise. It rained for days. The birds and animals fled to the mountains. The wooden people stayed right where they were. *[Right here we raised a wavy piece of blue cardboard to show the water rising.]*

MY PUPPET. It won't be long before those stupid wooden people are all dead.

MIRANDA'S PUPPET. I can't wait.

NARRATOR. Just then Heart of Earth saw something in the water. Heart of Heaven saw the same thing.

BOTH PUPPETS TOGETHER. They float! *[Wooden people happily floating along]*.

NARRATOR. Lightning scorched the ground. The earth quaked *[Theater shakes]*. And the wooden people lived. After the flood *[Water goes down]* the wooden people moved to the forest. Heart of Heaven sent hurricanes *[Sound of wind]*. Heart of Earth shook the ground *[Theater shakes]*, but no matter what they tried, Heart of Heaven and Heart of Earth could not frighten the wooden people.

BOTH OF OUR VOICES. Today the descendants of the wooden people still live high in the trees.

[Here Miranda pulled the cord for the special effect. The sheet above us slid open, and eight stuffed monkeys on strings flopped down and dangled above the puppets.]

BOTH OF OUR VOICES. They are the monkeys, who are scared of nothing and laugh at everyone, especially

Heart of Heaven and Heart of Earth, the two gods who let being a god go to their heads.

I pulled the cord that closed the little curtains. And the audience went wild.

My legs felt wobbly as Miranda and I dragged the puppet theater back behind the curtain. The audience was still clapping. Miranda was grinning and hopping and patting me. "They *loved* us! They *loved* us!" she kept saying. I managed to smile at her, but I couldn't say anything because I was still letting out my breath in big sighs. It was over.

All the way down our row of seats other kids poked us and said they liked the puppets. I felt like my face would freeze in a permanent grin just hearing it, even though I knew it wasn't for sure that we had won. By the time we got back to our seats the girls who were doing the dance were onstage. They were dressed like quetzal birds, with green leotards and long green crepe paper tails.

The music started and they circled around. LaRhonda Sims was the leader. She's been in ballet since she was five. The girls did different stuff, like getting captured, escaping, flying away. At the end they all died, I think, except one rose up at the very end like maybe she wasn't all the way dead. I think it was supposed to be a story, but I didn't get it. It was pretty and creative, and LaRhonda is really popular. The audience clapped like crazy for the quetzal bird dancers.

After the dance there were two speeches. Willie Barazzi's

was really good, because it was about why the Mayan civilization ended. No one knows for sure. It's just a lot of guessing, which makes it so mysterious. Missy Ratyzsck's speech was about the kind of food the Mayans ate. It was so boring and the way she talked, all breathy and sexy like she does, made it so hard to understand that I just wished she would hurry up. I don't see how anyone could make beans, squash, and fruit interesting. No one even clapped afterward. I felt sorry for her, but I was glad it was over. Now the winner would be announced. Miranda grabbed my hand and squeezed so hard it hurt.

Ms. Linstrom walked across the stage. She had a piece of paper in her hand. "I want to commend you all on the effort that went into each entry in the performance competition."

I bit my thumbnail. Now Miranda's fingers dug into my arm.

"It was difficult to choose between all the fine performances, and I want you to know that you are all winners in my book." Ms. Linstrom smiled.

I slumped down in my seat. Miranda leaned over and breathed on my cheek.

"Tomorrow," said Ms. Linstom, "the arts and crafts entries will be on display in the library." She lifted up the paper and adjusted her glasses.

"Third place," read Ms. Linstrom, "goes to the quetzal bird dancers." Everyone clapped. The girls got up and took their third-place ribbon. I was breathing hard.

"Second place goes to Willie Barazzi for his wonderful speech on the decline of Mayan civilization." Willie stood up and took a bow. Then he ran up the steps and got his red second-place ribbon. Everyone laughed and clapped. My armpits were totally soaked.

"And first place," said Ms. Linstrom (I held my breath), "goes to two very creative and hardworking girls. Let's all give a big hand to Miranda Evancich and Trina Stenkawsky for their delightful puppet show."

Miranda screamed right in my ear. She jumped up, jerking my arm and pulling me to my feet. She hugged me and waved to everyone in the auditorium. I felt my face go red. My legs were like Jell-O. Miranda had to drag me up the stairs and onto the stage, where Ms. Linstrom handed us a blue ribbon. "Nice job, girls," she said. "Good luck in the final judging."

"Students," said Ms. Linstrom. She clapped her hands to get our attention. "You may return to your classes now. Congratulations to all of you who won a ribbon. We'll see you at the Land of the Maya celebration and dance on Friday, the third of May, when the Cultural Arts Week grand prize winner will be chosen. Be sure to invite your parents. Good luck to all of you and good job."

The assembly was dismissed and all the kids went back to their classrooms. "Can you believe it?" squealed Miranda, right in my ear. She hugged me and hopped in a little circle, and her ponytail whopped me across the face, but I didn't mind. "I thought I'd *die* when she said our names! Wasn't it horrible waiting so long?" Miranda kept talking like that, sort of thinking out loud like she does. All I could think of was the blue ribbon in my hand. "And I'm so pitted out. Do you think anyone noticed? Do you think I stink?" She wasn't really asking for an answer. I felt too happy to talk. It was almost too hard to believe.

We had a chance to win! I'd never been to camp.

I looked over Miranda's shoulder at a group of droopy-looking kids, the ones who hadn't won. They weren't giggling and hanging on each other. The boys looked mad. I was too happy to feel sorry for them, but I sure can guess how they felt, like mud, or worse.

During math Miranda passed me a note. It said, "Meet me at the camp after school. Bring food. Congratulations, Puppet show girl no. 1." I wrote back and said O.K. After that school took forever to be over.

The house was quiet when I got home. I almost yelled about winning first place, but then I figured everyone must be napping, so instead I tiptoed around looking for Mom and Dad. Dad was snoozing on the couch, his face turned to the wall. The TV was on and someone was kissing someone else. It looked like they were Frenching. Mom was not around, and I didn't want to wake up Dad.

I went upstairs and found Mom on her bed. She opened her eyes when she saw me and put her finger to her lips because Marissa and Glendon were sleeping on her bed. I pulled out the blue ribbon and showed it to Mom.

She nodded and smiled, but that's it. I wanted to tell her all about it. I wanted to tell her about the boys popping bags of ketchup and the dancing girls dressed like green birds, how hard everyone clapped for us, how horrible it was sweating and waiting to find out, but she looked so tired. I could tell she didn't want to wake up the little kids, so I didn't say a word.

I pretended to ride a horse and she nodded, mouthed "See you later," and put her head back on the pillow with a little sigh. I tiptoed to my bedroom, changed my clothes, folded the ribbon carefully, and stuck it in my jeans pocket. Then I left to go catch Chico.

He was way out in the pasture, so I had to rattle the feed bin lid extra loud to get him to come. When he heard it his head popped straight up, and he came trotting to the barn. Priscilla came too, her huge milk bag swinging and bumping between her legs. She was giving oodles of milk these days, way more than we could use. And since there wasn't any calf to feed, we gave the extra to Mrs. Abrigo. She knows how to make cheese.

I gave them both a cupful of oats, then slipped the bridle up over Chico's nose and hopped on his back. He flicked me with his tail when I leaned over to unlatch the gate. We slid through, and Chico gave a little trot at the end so the gate wouldn't bang his rear end.

He knew where we were going, and I didn't have to use the reins much. I dug the ribbon out of my pocket. I smoothed its creases and spread it out on my leg.

It felt good to have that ribbon. But it didn't feel the same as right afterward, and it didn't feel the same as when I was running all the way home to tell someone. Dad was sure sleeping a lot these days. Mom was busy and tired and needed her naps, especially now that she was pregnant. Mom was happy for me, I could tell by her smile, but I wanted more. I'm not sure what, or maybe I am sure but it's hard to say it when you want your mom and dad to do something or be something that they aren't. I wanted them to care about our puppet-show blue ribbon like I cared, even if it was only a piece of shiny cloth, but they had been too busy resting.

I looked at the ribbon again. The gold printing that said FIRST PLACE was flaky in places. The bottom was starting to fray. I stuffed it back in my pocket.

Miranda was waiting at our camp. She'd brought sugar cubes for the horses, and we gave them their treats before we tied them. I sat down in the soft grass and Miranda flopped down beside me. "Look," she said, and pulled a huge bag of M&M's out of her backpack. "My mom said we had a lot to celebrate today because we won first place. Can you believe she gave me candy *before* dinner?"

We both laughed, and then Miranda crawled over and leaned against me. She dropped the bag of candy in my lap, put her arms around me, and hugged me really hard. I hugged her too, squishing my cheek against hers.

"We did it, we did it, we did it!" she whispered, and my grin almost split my face in two.

We hugged each other for a long time. My heart was so full of good feelings I could hardly stand it, and all I could think of was how great it is to be twelve and have a friend and a horse and a Land of the Maya blue ribbon and a whole bag of M&M's before dinner.

We tore open the bag and ate chocolate until we almost popped, first red for first prize (there aren't any blue), then green for sexiness (Miranda thinks they will give her boobs), then orange for Miranda's hair, tan for my hair, and brown for Chico and Tonka. We ate the yellows last. Yellow for the golden Land of the Maya medal the grand prize winners would get.

Miranda said we had to get new dresses for the dance afterward and asked if my mom would let me wear high heels and did I want to get shoes that matched. We rolled around, laughed, ate chocolate, hugged, looked at our ribbon, and dreamed about YMCA camp until it was time to go home for dinner.

By the time I got home it didn't matter so much that Mom and Dad had been too busy napping to get excited.

THE rest of the week flew by. Matt Soto and Billy Ray Blodgett won first place in the crafts division for their Mayan temple model. Julia Jenkins won first place in the art division for her painting of a Mayan city. Delayne Whitt won first place for his mystery story about a murdered Mayan priest. All of us sixth graders were put into committees for decorating the gym. During P.E. we had to practice waltzing. Another week went by. All of a sudden it was May.

I still didn't have a dress. Miranda kept saying her mom was going to take us shopping, but I didn't have any money and didn't want to ask for any either. Mom didn't ask what I was going to wear for the dance. In fact, I wasn't sure she was even planning to come, since she didn't say anything when I told her that all the parents were invited. Maybe it's because she was scrubbing green Kool-Aid out of the tablecloth when I told her.

I went through the dresses in my closet, looking for something dressy, but when you ride horses a lot and don't go to church or parties or weddings anymore you have a lot of jeans and T-shirts and not too many dresses. I decided to ask Miranda if I could borrow one of hers.

Dad was sleeping even more. When he wasn't sleeping

he was mad or gone. I don't know where he went. Mom kept saying, "Dad's back is really bothering him," and I felt sorry for him, but I was secretly so glad when I came home and found him sleeping (and not yelling or muttering) that I tried not to make too much noise whenever I was in the house, and I didn't ask for anything, especially not money. Borrowing a dress isn't such a big deal.

I helped Mom when I could. Sometimes I fixed dinner, and once in a while I changed diapers. There was tiredness on Mom's face even when she smiled, and I wished she didn't have to take care of other people's kids all the time. We didn't talk about our baby. It was like a secret that everyone knows but pretends they don't.

Then one day Mom was staring out the window and called me over. She took my hand and put it on her stomach, kind of toward the side and down low, and I felt a little something bump against my hand. It bumped, and then it pushed and stayed sticking out just for a second. I was so surprised that I held my breath. I asked Mom if it hurt, but she just smiled and said it was a wonderful feeling. She said, "Someday you'll understand," but right then I was hoping everything was O.K. in there.

Three days before May Day I still hadn't asked Miranda if I could borrow a dress. We'd been waltzing every day during P.E., and the boys had to be our partners. They hated the idea as much as we did and stepped on our feet on purpose. I got Brian Sorenson. He smells weird.

After school I went home with Miranda, and on the way I asked if I could borrow a dress. She said sure, so when we got to her house we looked through the closet. There were a lot of dresses in there. Miranda went downstairs to look for a snack, and I found a dress I liked, a pink one with a bow and a low, low back. I'd have to go without a bra, but it was fluffy enough in front that I didn't care.

When Miranda came back upstairs we practiced waltzing between eating potato chips. We took turns being the boy. We were dancing in Miranda's room saying one-two-three, one-two-three out loud when Mrs. Evancich called up and asked if we wanted to go shopping. Miranda jumped up and down, clapped, and stepped on my toe, just like Brian Sorenson.

"I have to be back by dinner," I said, but Mrs. Evancich told me to call my mom and ask if I could go out for dinner with them instead. Mom said yes and to be sure to say thank you, and we got in the car and drove to the mall. It hardly takes any time at all to get to the mall in a car. When I go with Mom we always take the bus, two buses really, and it takes so long that Mom never wants to go. Besides, we don't have the money to shop at the mall, so not having a car is a good excuse.

Mrs. Evancich parked the car in front of J. C. Penney, and we walked through the store without even stopping to look. Miranda kept skipping and poking me in that way of hers, but I'm used to it and I wasn't too embarrassed. I wondered what kind of dress Miranda would get, what color would go with that hair of hers.

We walked down the mall, and Mrs. Evancich's high

heels made a fast *clickety-clickety* all the way to Nordstrom's, the nicest, richest, and fanciest store in our mall. Inside it smelled of leather and new towels and perfume. We passed the shoe department and all the beautiful women at the makeup and jewelry counters. We passed the man in the black suit and bow tie playing the big black piano. We went up the escalator to the department that I call the Party Dress Department. Miranda knew where to go and pushed her way past racks of dresses until she found our size.

"Look at this, Mom!" she yelled, and a few people looked over at her. Mrs. Evancich and I squeezed between the full racks until we were at the size twelve rack. Miranda was already pushing the dresses along the rack, pulling out one and then another and holding them up to herself.

"Not a good color, Miranda," said Mrs. Evancich. Miranda held up another one. "No, no red. Absolutely not." Miranda stuck her tongue out and put the dress back. Then she pulled out a dress the color of a new peach. It was made in two layers, with shiny satin underneath and airy see-through stuff over the top. The sleeves were puffy. The skirt was fluffy and big but not like a little kid's dress. It had a black velvet belt around the waist that ended in a huge bow in the back. Miranda held it up to herself, and the peachy color of it, the beauty of it, made her look like an angel.

"That's gorgeous, honey," said Mrs. Evancich. "Go ahead and try it on."

Not *how much does it cost?* Not *let's look at a few others,* just *go ahead and try it on.*

I watched Miranda hop off to the dressing room and thought about the dress I had picked from her closet. It was a good one, not as fancy but good.

"Now let's find something for Trina," said Mrs. Evancich, and I felt my face go all hot and blotchy. She moved some dresses along the rack, looked at me with a squint, moved a few more dresses. I didn't have a dime. And if I did, it wouldn't have bought one of those dresses.

"I'm going to borrow a dress," I said. "I don't really need dresses much." She didn't even look at me. She pulled out a pink dress, and it was so beautiful I gasped.

"Oh, look," I said, wanting to touch it. She held it up to me, and I could hear and feel the swish of the cloth against my legs. I reached down and smoothed it with both hands. It was sleek and shiny, not puffy like Miranda's. It had a wide white collar, sort of like a sailor collar but not really, and about a million pleats that started at the waist and swooped down into a long, flowing skirt past my knees.

"This one would show off your figure nicely," said Mrs. Evancich. "You've got a nice figure already, Trina. Want to try it?" I blushed again and stared down at my tennis shoes. My own mom had never said anything about my figure. I'm not sure she even knew I wore a bra now. I had bought it with my own money. "Go try it on," said Mrs. Evancich.

It wouldn't have been polite to argue, so I took the dress over to the dressing room. I hung the dress on a hook in one of the little compartments and took off my clothes, my shoes too, because they would look so ugly with that dress. As I slipped the dress over my head I could hear Miranda humming in her dressing room. It was smooth and cool against my skin. I zipped it up and looked in the mirror. I could hardly believe what I saw.

"Hurry up!" said Miranda. She banged on the door of my dressing room until I came out. When she saw me she whistled the way boys do when they're acting smart, grabbed my hand, and danced me around.

"One-two-three, look at me! One-two-three, you're the queen!" she sang, until her mom said, "Miranda Elaine," and we both stepped out so she could see us.

"Perfect," said Mrs. Evancich with a great big smile. "What beautiful little girls you are."

"*Mom,*" said Miranda.

"Sorry, young *ladies,*" said Mrs. Evancich and then she said to the sales clerk. "We'll take them both."

I know my mouth fell open because Mrs. Evancich winked at me and said, "Don't gawk, dear," in a prissy way that wasn't scolding. I couldn't say a word, not a single word, so I shut my mouth. She'd bought me stuff before, just for fun, like the bridle for Chico, but a fancy dress? It was incredible. Miranda yanked me toward the dressing room.

"Happy birthday early," she whispered, and then she flung her arm around my neck, and we went to find our clothes.

By the time we were dressed the sales clerk had wrapped the dresses in boxes and put them in big purple bags that said NORDSTROM'S in white letters on one side. Mrs. Evancich held her arms around both of us and whispered, "Shoes?" and Miranda hopped once and practically ran to the down escalator.

Mrs. Evancich still had her arm around me. "Thanks," I mumbled. She squeezed me really hard and said I'd better hurry or Miranda would have all the shoe salespeople tied up and I wouldn't find a single thing I wanted. I rushed down the escalator, the purple bag banging against my leg. I didn't wait for the stairs to carry me down. I flew down two steps at a time.

We ended up with shoes that matched. And pantyhose that matched, my first pair. And then we went to McDonald's and ate as much as we wanted and got dessert too. When we pulled into our driveway I was full of hamburgers and ice cream and shopping and happiness and couldn't wait to show Mom and Dad my new dress. I told Mrs. Evancich thanks again, that it was the best dress I'd ever had, which is true. Miranda said she'd see me tomorrow, and I went inside to find Mom.

The day-care kids were gone, so it was quiet. I found Mom watching TV in the dark. Dad wasn't on the couch.

"Look what I got!" I said, but when she turned to face me her eyes were all puffy and red and so was her nose, and even though she smiled at me everything was wrong. I put the bag behind me, but it was too big to hide, so I just sort of swung it in front of me like it was nothing.

"We just went to the mall," I said. "No big deal." She looked at the TV and nodded. "Where's Dad?" I asked.

"He went out. He said he wanted some fresh air." She didn't say where. She didn't ask what was in my bag. "Do you have any homework tonight?" I shook my head, but she didn't see me because she was looking at the TV again. I crossed the room and kissed her on the cheek. It was damp.

"What's wrong, Mom?" I asked.

"Dad's back has been really bothering him," she said, "but it's nothing for you to worry about."

For a second I felt sort of mad. That wasn't it and I knew it. She was keeping something from me. Mom was always so protective, probably because I had been an only child for so long. Why couldn't she tell me what was going on? It didn't seem fair. I wanted to yell at her, make her tell me the truth. I almost did, but her face was so horribly sad.

"I'll see you in the morning, Mom," I said instead. "I love you."

"I know," whispered Mom, and then I left really quickly because I felt so awful inside. I had a million questions. And there was no way I could ask her any of them.

I know it's not his back. Is it because of the baby? The baby that nobody talks about? Is that why Dad sleeps all the time? Is that why he goes out at night?

The purple shopping bag was heavy. I tossed it into a chair and changed into pajamas without taking a shower. *What's the big hurry?* I asked myself. I could show them the dress on the night of the dance. It would be a surprise for everyone.

The box was taped shut. I didn't open it. I didn't feel like looking at my new dress. I left in on the chair. I pulled the covers up to my chin and flipped out the light, but I didn't go to sleep for a long, long time.

In the middle of the night I woke up when the front door slammed. Dad. I looked at my clock. It was three-thirty. I heard him come up the stairs and undress in the other room. He mumbled something, and I heard Mom mumble something. Then I didn't hear anything until the robins started up again.

DAD stayed out late the next couple of nights too, but Mom didn't talk about it and I didn't ask. I told her about the dance coming up, about the awards, just to try to get her mind off Dad, but she didn't seem interested. I told her at least six times that the parents were invited. She hardly seemed to hear me. Miranda and I practiced waltzing every day. It took my mind off things at home, a little anyway.

The frog in my stomach woke me up on the day of the dance. I awoke fast, without any of the groggy, lazy time I usually have in bed every morning. My first thought was the awards ceremony. That got my heart pumping and my stomach jumping like crazy. I hardly ate a bite of breakfast. There just wasn't room down there.

School was boring except when Brian Sorenson accidentally threw his retainer in the garbage can during lunch and had to dig through hot dogs and chili and crusts looking for it. He found it, but I noticed he didn't have it on when we were practicing waltzing. He stepped on my foot only three times.

After school Miranda and I stayed to help decorate the gym. Mr. Durkovic had us paint palm trees and toucans on big sheets of paper, and we hung them on the walls with long strips of masking tape. Then we helped two other girls make a big sign that said LAND OF THE MAYA and taped about a hundred balloons all around it.

I'd had a bad pain in my middle all day, a sort of ache and diarrhea feeling that made me wonder if I was getting sick. I tried not to think about the program and the dance too much, like who would win the grand prize, but being in the gym all decorated with posters of temples and jungle, thinking about dancing and my dress and what was going to happen, what *might* happen, was all too much. My stomachache got worse. A couple of times it hurt so much I could hardly stand up straight.

For two weeks I'd tried not to bite my nails. Miranda was going to borrow a really good color of nail polish from her mom, and we planned to have matching nails, but by four-thirty most of the posters were hung and all of my fingernails were gone. Miranda noticed right away. She shook her head and said she'd walk me home.

"Why don't you just stop biting them?" she asked. We took the long way, down the avenue and up the steep hill that was our street.

"I don't know," I said. "I don't think about it. It just happens when I'm nervous." My stomach hurt and my fingers hurt and I was mad at myself for doing it. I was mad at Miranda for noticing.

"Mom says you're really a nervous kid," said Miranda.

"I'm not either," I snapped. I felt like she'd smacked me. Why would Mrs. Evancich say that? "I'm just nervous today, about tonight."

"Well they look gross, like bloody stumps." Miranda picked a dandelion and stuck it under my chin. "Do you like butter?"

"Shut up, Miranda!"

We walked up the hill together, not talking. I looked sideways. Miranda's shoulders drooped. She didn't bounce. "Sorry," she said finally. Then she stopped in her tracks and grabbed me by the shoulders. "Hey! We could go to the drugstore and get you some of those glue-on nails! The long, wicked-looking ones. No one will know." She waggled her fingers stiffly, like she had long, long nails and didn't want to touch anything. "Dahling, do you like them? They're real, you know."

The anger slid away and I smiled. "I think I'll stick to my bloody stumps, thanks," I said, and we both cracked up.

"My mom will drive us just before seven," said Miranda. She skipped and got ahead, then turned around and walked backward to talk to me, and then skipped and bounced some more. "My dad will come later in the other car. Are your mom and dad coming?"

"Sure," I said, but I wasn't sure, especially about Dad.

Miranda chattered and skipped and asked if I was going to curl my hair, and then she said, "Oh yeah, your hair is already curly!" and giggled at her own dumb mistake.

When we got to my house Miranda said, "Bye! See you later!" and ran off down the alley. I went in to find Mom. She was washing dishes at the kitchen sink and humming what sounded like "I'm a Little Teapot." That's what she gets for hanging out with little kids all the time. I put my arms around her and hugged her from behind. The baby poked out in front a little more than the last time.

"How was school?" she asked. Glendon grabbed my jeans and begged to be picked up. I picked him up, kissed him on the cheek, and sat him on my hip the way Mom does. He stuck one finger in my ear.

"It was okay," I said, pulling Glendon's finger out of my ear. "I was pretty nervous all day."

"About what?" asked Mom. Marissa opened the fridge. "Close the refrigerator door, Marissa," said Mom.

"The awards program is tonight," I said. "And the dance. Remember I told you about them?" I waited for her to say something. She scrubbed a pot with a steel wool pad. She didn't even look at me. "Are you going to come?" I asked. Marissa pulled out the vegetable drawer and took out a head of lettuce.

"Oh, that's right," said Mom, and then she wiped her hands on a dish towel, took the lettuce away from Marissa, and shut the refrigerator door. "Don't worry, I didn't forget," she said. I didn't believe her. Just then Wayne called from the bathroom.

"Come wipe me!"

"Just a minute," called Mom. "What time does it start?"

"Eight," I said. "I have to be there early. Miranda's mom will pick me up."

"Great," said Mom. "I can't wait to see you." Then she headed for the bathroom. I grabbed an apple from a bowl on the counter and went outside to clean the barn.

As soon as Chico and Priscilla heard me in the barn they came looking for handouts. They stuck their heads over the half door into the barn and looked so pitiful that I gave in and poured them a little grain. I scooped out their stalls, broke open a new bale of straw, and spread it in a thick layer over the barn floor. Then I let Chico in for his dinner but made Priscilla stay out because she doesn't get her dinner until Dad milks her.

The first thing I noticed when I got back in the house was the smell. Someone had barfed. I wasn't the only person who was feeling rotten that day. Wayne was in the bathroom crying and Mom was in there with him saying, "It's okay, Waynie, I bet you feel better now." Mister Rogers was singing in the living room, something about saying no to strangers.

Wayne had barfed on the couch. That's where the smell was coming from. The little kids didn't seem to mind it. They were sprawled on the floor watching some puppets talk to a grown up guy dressed like a dog. Wayne came in looking pale. He had a plastic ice cream carton in his arms, our family barf bucket. He climbed into the rocking chair and hugged the bucket like a teddy bear. Mom came in with a rag and started scrubbing. I held my nose and watched TV.

"Where's Dad?" I asked, breathing through my mouth. Dad wasn't going to like that smell all over his couch.

"Didn't you see him when you were in the barn?" she asked. "He said he was going out to the garden." She held the rag high in one hand, with the other hand under it in case any chunks fell off, and went back in the bathroom to rinse the rag. I closed my eyes and swallowed. Barf is ten times worse than poop.

"He wasn't out there," I said. "What's for dinner?"

"Would you open a couple of cans of soup for me?" Mom called from the bathroom. "And make some toast."

"Sure," I said. Anything to get away from that smell. Mom came back with the rag and started to scrub again. A little trolley tooted and chugged across the TV screen. I went out to the kitchen. I was still breathing from my mouth. It takes about five minutes to heat canned soup and five more to make toast and set the table and get the milk out. I looked at the clock. It was five-thirty. I had an hour and a half to eat and get ready. "I'll go get Dad," I yelled, and ran outside.

The garden is behind the barn. It's really huge for a family garden. Dad plants all kinds of things out there, like tomatoes and lettuce and corn and three kinds of beans and potatoes and carrots. When I was little he would let me put the seeds in the ground and spread the dirt over the top. Then we'd stomp the dirt down with our feet and sing, "Here come the elephants, here come the elephants." I still remember him laughing at how small my footprints were compared with his.

"You aren't much of an elephant," he'd say, then he'd pick me up, kiss me, and poke me in the nose with a dirty finger. Dad never slept back then, except at night.

I looked all over for Dad. He wasn't in the garden. I looked in the barn, but all I saw was Chico munching away at his oats. I thought maybe Dad was in the toolshed, so I went there next.

"Dad?" I called. And that's when I found him. He was lying on his side in the dirt beside the toolshed.

"Dad! Are you okay?" I ran to him. I bent over him and patted him, pounded him. My heart jumped in my throat and made my chest feel tight, and my hands were as cold as ice. I yelled "Dad! *Dad!*"

He rolled over to his back and looked up at me. His eyes were so dull and scary and far away that I could hardly breathe.

"What do you want, Trina." His voice didn't sound like his own. It was not like a live person's voice.

"Dinner, Dad." I was breathing hard, like I'd run a long way. My dad blinked a couple of times and groaned.

"I'm not hungry. Leave me alone."

"*Please,* Dad," I said. "Come in the house. Mom's waiting for you." I took one of his big rough hands and pulled on it. It was cold and the fingernails were dirty. He groaned again and sat up. He ran one hand over his hair and messed it up. Then he stood up in front of me, tall and horrible and so different from the dad who used to make elephant feet. He didn't say a word. He just went in the house and sat down at the table. He didn't even wash his hands. He didn't eat. He just sat there.

Mom kept the kids quiet. Glendon was already gone, and Wayne was pretty quiet because he didn't feel well. Marissa slurped her soup and didn't scream about a single thing. I tried to eat, but all I could think about was Dad sitting across from me and not eating, Dad lying on the ground in the dirt like a—I couldn't even think the word. The soup was awful and my stomach was hurting.

All of a sudden I remembered the program. The clock said six. I pushed my chair back and rushed upstairs. "I have to be ready in less than an hour," I yelled down to Mom. She didn't say anything.

I took a five-minute shower and dried off fast. Then I put on my underwear and wiped a clear place on the mirror. I combed my hair into a ponytail and slicked back the fuzzy curls around my face with Mom's pink goop. Then I hurried to my room and found the purple bag with my dress and shoes in it. I untaped the dress box and pulled off the lid. There was my dress, my pink, fancy, gorgeous, wonderful dress. It was wrapped in tissue paper and folded neatly. I unfolded it, and it didn't have a single wrinkle, which is a lucky thing because there wasn't time to iron anyway. I dug around in my desk for a pair of scissors and clipped off the tags. The price had been torn off, but there were still a lot of tags.

I slipped the dress over my head and felt the cool, smooth cloth slide all the way down. I'd forgotten about the pantyhose. I don't know whether you're supposed to put them on first or last. I wiggled into them, trying hard not to mess up my dress. It was hard to keep the legs from twisting. Then I took my new shoes out of the box and put them on.

There is a long mirror on the inside of my closet door, the kind you can see your whole self in. I stood in front of it and twirled around. I bowed to myself and looked at the clock. Half an hour to go. Miranda said she'd pick me up at a quarter to seven. I heard Mom saying good-bye to Wayne and Marissa downstairs and the door shutting. I grinned and curtsied to myself one more time, my princess self, and went downstairs.

Mom was already cleaning up. Dad was sitting at the table, his head in his hands. He hadn't eaten his soup, and it was still there, cold and greasy-looking. When I was little he used to call me princess. Tonight I even looked like one. I hoped he'd like my dress.

"How do you like it?" I asked. Mom turned around. Dad looked up. I twirled so they could see the skirt fluff out.

"You're gorgeous!" said Mom. She smiled. All her teeth showed, and her eyes were crinkly with happiness. "Where did you ever get that dress?"

"Mrs. Evancich bought it for me," I said. I twirled again. "It's an early birthday present."

Mom wiped her hands on a dish towel and crossed the room. She pushed some hair out of her eyes and stared at me. "What a wonderful birthday present." She took my hands in hers and stood back to look some more. "What nice people. I hope you told her thank you."

"What do you *think*?" I asked, pretending to be insulted, then we both laughed. Mom glanced up at the wall clock.

"I'd better hurry too," she said. Then she put one hand on my cheek and held it there like she just couldn't stop looking at me. I was grinning so hard my face hurt. Mom and I just looked at each other like that until I heard Dad get out of his chair.

"Take it off." He was looking down at my dress, and his eyes were as cold as two gray stones.

"I said take it *off!*" Dad's voice was loud and his face was red. My legs twitched and I felt cold all over. "No kid of mine is taking charity from a bunch of rich snobs!" Mom turned all the way around and looked at Dad.

"It's a birthday present, Mitch." Her voice was the one she uses when Marissa throws a tantrum, low, careful, even.

"Trina's birthday isn't until October." He was shaking now, and the veins on his neck stuck out like worms. "I said take that dress off now!" I jumped like he'd hit me. Tears blurred my eyes, until Dad looked like a blue smear with a skin-colored blob on top. Mom put her hands on my shoulders and turned me around.

"Go upstairs," she said.

I ran into my room, threw myself on the bed, and bawled. How could my own dad be so awful? I didn't have another dress, not a nice one, and it was too late to borrow one from Miranda, and how would I explain it anyway? I sobbed into my pillow and my whole bed shook.

Dad yelled some more, but I don't know what he said. The front door slammed. I heard Mom come up the stairs. She knocked on my door, but I didn't say anything. I couldn't say anything because I was crying too hard. She turned the doorknob and came in. I felt her sit down on the bed beside me. She put her hand on my back and just sat there with me and then finally said, "I think you're going to need this." I wiped my eyes on my pillow and turned over to see. She had a shiny pink ribbon in her hand. "It's for your hair. I bought it last time I went to the drugstore." She reached over and tied the ribbon around my ponytail. Then with her hand she smoothed the fuzzy curls that were already sticking out around my face. She hadn't forgotten.

"Go wash your face," said Mom. "Miranda will be here any minute."

"But Dad said—" and I couldn't finish because big sobs bubbled up from my throat. Mom put her arms around me. I buried my face on her shoulder and she went "shush, shush," the way she does with Marissa and Glendon.

"Daddy isn't feeling well these days," said Mom quietly. I remembered Wayne and the barf on the couch. And I thought of Dad lying on the ground and staring and then not eating his dinner.

"Did he get it from Wayne?" I asked, but I think even then I knew she wasn't talking about the flu.

"No," said Mom, "but you don't need to worry about it right now." She pulled me up, and we stood there looking at each other, me in my dress, her in jeans and a baggy shirt hanging down over the baby bump. "You just need to get ready for the program, and so do I." She looked down at herself and grinned. "You don't want me to show up looking like this, do you?"

I smiled back at her and wiped my nose on my hand. "I'll have to milk Priscilla tonight," said Mom, "but that won't take long. I might be a little late, but I'll be there." She turned me around and pushed me toward the bathroom. "Now go wash. Go, go, *go!*"

Just then a car honked outside. I splashed cold water on my face and dried it fast, wishing the water could wash away the tired, mixed-up ache in my heart. Then I ran down the stairs and out the door. "See you later, Mom!" I yelled.

Miranda was waiting in the back seat for me. I climbed in beside her, and the first thing she said was, "How come you're crying?"

"I'm just nervous." I lied. "And my stomach hurts a little." And of course Miranda started telling me all about how nervous she was and how gross dancing with boys was and how she could hardly eat her dinner and how she'd had to promise her brother Terry a week's worth of washing *and* drying so he wouldn't boo when we walked across the stage to get the grand prize. She made all these funny faces while she talked and bounced so hard in her seat that her mom twice had to say "Miranda Elaine." Once we got to school I was laughing so hard I almost forgot about my dad and my stomach.

By the time we walked up the steps and into the school building the only thing I could think of was the Land of the Maya dance and who would win the grand prize.

EVERYONE who had won any kind of a ribbon during Cultural Arts Week had to sit in the front two rows of the auditorium. Ms. Linstrom arranged us according to the event we'd won. We were all dressed up, even the boys. Miranda was on one side of me, LaRhonda and the other dancer girls on the other. Everyone was chattering. Two of the boys were doing burping noises under their armpits, until Mr. Durkovic made them quit. My hands were freezing and sweating at the same time.

Mr. Durkovic looked really different all dressed up. Every time he walked past me a cloud of cologne smell went up my nose. I was so nervous I couldn't talk, which was a good thing because a lot of kids were getting yelled at for making too much noise when they were supposed to be listening. Ms. Linstrom read us the program. The grand prize would be last, after the band and choir.

Pretty soon other people started to come. At first it was just a few families here and there. I looked for Mom. More families came and the auditorium got noisy. Miranda grabbed my hand.

"This is *it*," she said. She bounced around in her seat, looking around at the audience, turning this way and that.

"I'm so nervous I can't stand it." I nodded. It was all I could do to keep myself from jumping up and running out. My stomach churned.

It was nice to have Miranda near. She looked beautiful in her peachy, fluffy dress. She had curled her hair and it was puffy all around her face like a fiery cloud, and she didn't look like a kid anymore. Finally the lights went down. Even Miranda was quiet.

Ms. Linstrom walked across the stage and gave a little speech about Cultural Arts Week. Then she introduced Mr. Levi, the choir teacher, and the choir kids came down the aisles. I turned around to watch. There were moms whispering, little kids waving, and flashes of light, and there were even a few video cameras. All I could think of was needing to go to the bathroom. I looked around for my mom, but it was pretty dark and I couldn't see her.

The choir sang "Rocka My Soul in the Bosom of Abraham," "I'm a Yankee Doodle Dandy," and "Yellow Submarine." They sang some stuff I don't remember the names of, classical music, I think. Then they went down, and we all waited while the janitors took down the risers.

Ms. Linstrom introduced Mrs. Wiley, the band teacher, and all the band kids came onstage with their instruments. They played a march, "Take Me Out to the Ball Game," and what sounded like music from *Batman*. One kid played a solo on the trumpet. I wanted to cover my ears, it was so bad. There was lots of clapping and flashing, and when the band kids were done Ms. Linstrom stood in front and everyone got real quiet.

She told everyone about the different competitions for Cultural Arts Week, that all the sixth graders had been involved, and how hard everyone had worked. She told about the different categories and how they'd been judged. My stomach felt about the size of a golf ball. Finally she said she was going to introduce all the ribbon winners from each category, then give a special gift to each person, and then, *and then!* the grand prize would be awarded.

My heart was pounding. The art kids went up first. Each kid got a trophy. Julia Jenkins stayed onstage. Everyone clapped. I was breathing faster now. Next the kids who had written stories went up. They all got little trophies too. Delayne stayed up. Miranda linked her arm through mine and squeezed. Next the kids who had built models went up. Matt and Billy Ray stayed.

Miranda pulled me to my feet. We walked onstage together. The lights were hot, and I couldn't see a single face in the audience. Ms. Linstrom said some stuff about the performances. I didn't hear what she said. She handed each of us a little trophy. It was a gold cup on a heavy metal base. It shook in my hand. There was a lot of clapping and flashing. Then the other performance kids, the dancers and Willie Barazzi, left the stage, and everything was dead quiet.

"Each year," said Ms. Linstrom, "a special grand prize is awarded to the student or students whose entry in the Cultural Arts Week competition goes above and beyond even the most outstanding work of the other students." Miranda had her arm around my neck. She was jiggling up and down.

"We look at creativity, appropriateness to the theme, the amount of work that went into the project, and the overall enthusiasm of the students." Ms. Linstrom cleared her throat. She turned and talked to us. "All of you have done an outstanding job. I am only sorry we cannot award each of you the same grand prize. Thanks for your hard work, all of you."

I needed to swallow but I couldn't. I held my breath. My heart thumped in my throat.

"I am happy to say that this year's grand prize winners, for an outstanding and delightful dramatic presentation, are Miranda Elaine Evancich and Katherine Jean Stenkawsky!"

My name! My whole, long name and she said it right!

Lights flashed, people clapped. Miranda wrapped her arms around me and hopped up and down. Ms. Linstrom put a gold medal around our neck, mine first, then Miranda's. I looked at mine. It said CULTURAL ARTS WEEK, GRAND PRIZE WINNER. I looked at Miranda just in time to see her kiss her medal. We walked off the stage together. People were clapping, I was grinning, and Miranda was bouncing beside me.

We went down the steps of the stage, up the aisles, and out into the hall, like Mr. Durkovic had told us to do. Then we all went straight to the gym, where we had to get ready to do the Land of the Maya waltz, like we'd been doing in P.E. class. As soon as we got to the gym all the boys started faking slam dunks at the basketball hoops while the girls huddled around me and Miranda and wanted to see our medals.

Miranda skipped over to me and hugged me, actually more like jumped on me. She put her arms around me, and her medal poked me in the chest but not hard. "We did it! We did it!" she shouted. *"Yippeeee!"*

"Did you see my mom?" I asked.

"No, I didn't see anyone, and I didn't hear Terry boo either!" She twirled her big skirt around. "This is the best night of my life!" She grabbed my hands. "Isn't this the best night of your whole life, Trina?"

"It's pretty great." I was so happy about winning that I didn't want to think about the other stuff, I mean Dad and how mad he was about the dress. Funny how sometimes you can't stop thinking about something even when you wish you could.

By this time the parents and brothers and sisters and other teachers and friends were gathered all around the gym. I looked for my mom but didn't see her. Brian Sorenson came and grabbed my elbow. I said bye to Miranda and the music began. The talking stopped and the lights went out except for one big one right in the middle of the gym on the ceiling. All the sixth graders got ready to dance.

Once-two-three, one-two-three, we danced around kind of boxy-like. Brian didn't step on my toe once. Pretty soon some parents and a couple of teachers started waltzing. Ms. Linstrom danced with Mr. Durkovic. I wondered if they liked each other.

The music went on and on, and I didn't even have to count because the one-two-three was in my heart and in my head. Brian and I floated around and around. Pretty soon we weren't boxy at all. It was the best waltz of my life. More lights came on and more people joined in the dance, mostly grown-ups. I knew that the song was almost over, so I started looking around for my mom. I saw Mr. and Mrs. Evancich and Terry but not my mom. She was probably behind taller people. I couldn't wait to show her my gold medal.

Brian stepped on my foot really hard. I didn't yell but I did look down. That's when I saw the spots of blood on my shoes and down the legs of my first pair of pantyhose. I froze in one spot with my legs together. Brian jerked me once, but then the music ended and he ran to find his friends.

People crowded all around me, pushing and talking, and I couldn't move. How could I? If I went anywhere I'd drip blood and make a trail. I blinked and blinked so the tears wouldn't spill over. Miranda found me standing there like that. Her mom and dad were with her. I was totally paralyzed. "Are you okay?" asked Mrs. Evancich. I shook my head but didn't dare look down because I didn't want anyone else to look down and see it.

Mrs. Evancich took my arm and led me toward the bathroom, with Miranda skipping along behind and patting my shoulder. My neck was hot and my face was pounding. I prayed that no one saw the drips. Where was Mom?

When we got to the bathroom I rushed into a stall, slammed the door and started to cry. "What's wrong?" asked Miranda. She banged on the door. "What's *wrong?*"

"Nothing!" I yelled. I didn't mean to yell but it came out that way.

Mrs. Evancich said "Miranda Elaine," and then I heard Miranda's hippity-hoppity footsteps. The doors to the bathroom swung open and shut, and it was quiet.

"It's just me," said Mrs. Evancich, and her voice was soft and warm. "Are you sick, honey?"

"No," I sobbed. My stomach hurt, but it wasn't the sick kind of hurt.

"Can you tell me what's wrong?"

"My *period*," I sputtered, and then I started to cry hard. I didn't like telling someone else's mom about my period, even if it was Mrs. Evancich. Some things are private. I heard her purse snap open, and she handed me a pad under the stall door.

"Is it the first time, Trina?" she asked in that same, warm voice.

"No," I said, stripping off my bloody things and cleaning myself with toilet paper. "The second."

I had started in February, the day after Valentine's Day. Then in March and April nothing happened, so I had quit thinking about it all the time. I didn't tell anyone, not even Miranda, *especially* not blabbermouth Miranda. I wasn't ready for the whole world to know my secret, even if it was a good one. I didn't even tell Mom, but I think she guessed, because a couple days after I started she gave me five dollars for no reason, just in case I needed anything.

"Hand me out your pantyhose and undies," said Mrs. Evancich, and the way she said it made me feel not so embarrassed. I wadded them up and handed them over, and then I heard the water running. I heard her pull the towel roll around and around, and pretty soon she handed my things back to me.

"The pad will stick even if your underwear is damp," she

said. I said thanks and put on wet underpants, damp pantyhose, and my shoes and went out. I felt cold and gross and
wondered if anyone would be able to tell that I had wet
underwear on.

Mrs. Evancich put one arm around me and squeezed.
"I won't tell a soul," she whispered, and the way she said
"soul" made me sure she meant Miranda. Then she said,
"You look absolutely beautiful, Trina." I sniffed and said
thanks. I didn't want to talk about periods anymore.

"Your mom called right before we left the house," said
Mrs. Evancich. I wondered why Mom would call the Evanciches, and my heart started beating fast enough for me to hear
it. "She said to tell you that something came up and that she
wouldn't be able to make it tonight, but to tell you good luck
and give you a hug."

Mom didn't come. I felt like someone had slammed the
heavy bathroom door in my face. She didn't hear Ms. Linstrom
say our last name right. She didn't know Miranda and I were
the grand prize winners. She didn't see me get my gold
medal or waltz with Brian Sorenson.

"That's okay." I lied. "She's pretty tired these days." Mrs.
Evancich gave me a squeeze.

"Bob took a lot of pictures. We'll be sure you get some
to show her." I said thanks again. *Thanks for taking lots of
pictures. Thanks for washing my things and giving me a pad
that sticks to wet underpants. Thanks for the dress, the beautiful, wonderful princess dress.*

I wanted my mom. My own mom. Tears started dribbling
down my face again, and Mrs. Evancich saw.

"You girls have had a long, exhausting day," she said. "I'll go find Miranda and take you both home, okay?" I nodded and she went into the noise and crowds of the gym, and for the second time that night I washed my face in cold water.

10

Miranda talked all the way home. I didn't hear a thing she said.

When I got home I found Mom sitting in the rocking chair in front of the TV, but the TV wasn't on. Dad wasn't around. I was glad. I didn't want him to see me in the dress. Mom just sat there rocking and rocking. She didn't even hear me until I said hi.

"Sorry I couldn't make it, Trina," she said, but she didn't look at me. She just kept rocking. I took my gold medal off. "Did you have a good time?" she asked, still rocking.

"I guess so." I didn't show her the medal. I didn't tell her about winning. She didn't ask. "Brian Sorenson only stepped on my foot once." I didn't tell her what I saw when he did it.

Mom rubbed the baby bump and sighed. I waited for something to happen, for her to say something, to ask me who won, who got the free week at camp, and did the gym look good all decorated with posters?

The clock on the mantel went *clip-clip-clip* and almost matched the rocking-chair sound. My underwear was damp and warm. Mrs. Evancich's pad was thick and hot between my legs. I bit my lip. I wanted to shake my mom. *Why weren't you there to wash out my first pair of pantyhose?* I wanted to shake her and scream in her face. *Look at me! Notice me! I'm a grand prize winner!*

Mom must have heard the yelling in my mind. She turned and looked at me. Her eyes squinted because of the light behind me, and her face looked more covered with wrinkles than ever before.

"Dad's in the hospital." Her voice was only a whisper. "I just got home."

"What happened?" I sank to the floor beside her and hung on to the chair. My gold medal dropped out of my hand. The ribbon lay under one of the rockers, but suddenly I didn't care. All my mad feelings toward Mom disappeared the way a soap bubble pops when it lands in the grass. "Is he okay?"

"After you left I went to look for him," said Mom. "When I found him he—" She stopped, like she couldn't say more.

"*What* Mom?" I asked, shaking her arm. "What happened?" Had she found him on the ground too? I hadn't told her about that.

"He wasn't himself." She bit her lower lip and tried to blink the tears away. "He frightened me. I called Father Tom. I didn't know what else to do."

He frightened me too. I didn't say it out loud.

"Father Tom drove us to the hospital. They said Dad needs to rest for a few days."

"Mom," I said, "what's wrong with him?" I shook her arm, begging her to tell me.

"Some sort of a nervous breakdown or something." She

didn't look at me when she said it. Was that all? What did it mean? "What Dad needs most is plenty of rest." Mom patted my hand.

More rest? Ever since the crippled calf was born, ever since we'd found out about the baby, Dad had slept most of the time. How could he need more rest? It didn't make sense. And why had she called Father Tom? We hadn't been to church in more than a year. Why didn't she call the Abrigos or an ambulance? What happens when someone has a nervous breakdown?

"When can he come home?" I asked.

"The doctor said he'll call me tomorrow," said Mom. "Then we'll know more." She reached over and put her arm around my shoulders. "Try not to worry," she said. "Everything will work out." She rubbed the baby bump again, and I wondered if the baby was wiggling in there.

"Go on up to bed, Trina," said Mom. "It's late."

I fished the gold medal out from under the rocker. Mom saw it. "Did you get that tonight?" she asked.

"Yes," I said. "Miranda and I won the grand prize."

"That's wonderful, Trina Jean," said Mom. "I'm so sorry I missed it."

"It wasn't any big deal, Mom," I said, choking on the words. She already felt terrible, about Dad, about missing the program. I could tell by the tears spilling out of her eyes and running down her cheeks. How could I tell her what really happened? It would only make her feel worse.

I went upstairs to bed. I stripped off my clothes, threw my new dress on a chair, and took a long, hot shower. I scrubbed and scrubbed. I washed away the stickiness of blood, the sweaty nervousness of being a Cultural Arts Week grand prize winner, the smell of Brian Sorenson.

I scrubbed at the anger, the confusion, the scared, sick feeling I had about Dad. I thought maybe if I scrubbed hard enough, if I used enough soap, the feelings would go away, like dirty water down the drain. But when I finally turned off the water and dried myself, I felt as loaded down and smothered and mixed-up as before.

I didn't go to sleep for a long time. The wonderful, thrilling feelings about winning the grand prize had disappeared, and all I could think about was Dad. He wasn't my dad anymore. Not like he used to be. He was different now and scary. I thought about him sleeping in a hospital bed, and what I thought next surprised me and made my heart jump up into my throat. I hoped he'd stay there for a long, long time.

DAD was in the hospital for three weeks. He couldn't have any visitors, not even Mom. It wasn't like when he hurt his back. Then we got to visit him every day and I sneaked him beer nuts and Cheese Doritos and he was always glad to see me. I knew exactly what was wrong with him then.

No one would tell me what exactly a nervous breakdown was. All Mom said was that Dad needed peace and quiet. He was resting in the hospital. He was taking special medicine to help him feel better. When he came back he would be more like himself.

When she said these things, Mom always forced herself to smile, trying to persuade me that everything was fine. I didn't want Mom to worry, so I pretended to be excited about Dad coming home. I didn't tell her what I secretly wished— that he would stay away longer.

Everything was different without Dad. For one thing, he wasn't lying around sleeping all the time, so we didn't have to be so careful. I didn't have to tiptoe and worry about whether to wake him for dinner or not or keep the TV turned down low. Mom hardly shushed the kids at all. For three whole weeks no one was mad. There wasn't any yelling. Mom was tired, and sometimes I caught her with that worried look on her face, staring out into space and day-dreaming, but without Dad around she started to laugh out loud about things again. That was really great.

You don't realize how much you miss something, like the sound of Mom's laughter, until it's gone for a long time and comes back all of a sudden. Every time she laughed I laughed too, like when Marissa wore Mom's fuzzy blue slippers and told us she had Cookie Monster feet. Or when she dumped Wayne's jar of tadpoles into the toilet and we had to fish them out with our hands while Wayne was screaming and Marissa was saying, "Fwoggies in the potty." When Mom laughed she didn't look tired at all.

I graduated from sixth grade on May 21, and Mom and Mr. and Mrs. Abrigo came to watch. I wore my Land of the Maya dress, but it didn't feel as beautiful as before. Even though I knew how much Dad needed his rest in the hospital, graduating without him gave me an empty feeling. I wondered what it would be like when he came home.

Mr. and Mrs. Abrigo took us out for dinner afterward. Mom and I laughed at Mr. Abrigo's stories about Italy. Mrs. Abrigo told me to choose any dessert I wanted. I picked cheesecake with cherries on top, even though I was full. It would have been rude to hurt her feelings. I wished Dad hadn't missed my graduation.

Miranda and I went to our camp a couple of times. We sang camp songs and talked about going to YMCA camp in August. It's funny, but as much as I love riding and being with Miranda, as much as I wanted to get excited about YMCA camp, I wanted to be with Mom even more. I didn't have that feeling of wanting to get out of the house all the time. So when Mom needed me, to help with kids or to milk Priscilla or whatever, I wanted to be there with her. She was getting fatter and looking pretty tired. She needed me most of the time.

Glendon's mom brought Trinidad a couple of days after school was out. It was good to have four kids again, even though it was like a zoo around the house. With Dad gone it was extra noisy, but I didn't mind, because I wasn't worried all the time about him yelling. We'd been eating a lot of soup and toast. We needed the money. And it kept Mom and me busy.

Right after school let out Mom promised to pay me five dollars a week for helping her with the kids while Dad was in the hospital. So every morning after I milked Priscilla I made sandwiches and Kool-Aid and put them in the fridge for later. Then when all the kids were watching "Sesame Street" and "Mister Rogers' Neighborhood," Mom would go see Father Tom over at the church.

At first I thought she was going to Mass, until Miranda said that Mass starts at six in the morning on weekdays and only really old people go, like Mrs. Abrigo. When I asked her, Mom said she and Father Tom just talked. That's all she said. When she came back she always seemed less tired, stronger somehow on the inside. I could see it in her eyes and in the way she held her head. Seeing Father Tom was good for Mom.

It would have been nice to have someone to talk to like that. I didn't tell Miranda anything except that Dad was sick.

That's all I knew for sure anyway. And even if I'd known, I might not have told her. Her family is perfect. I knew she wouldn't understand.

I thought about Dad most of the time. I worried about Mom and tried hard to take good care of her, to help her with the kids as much as I could. Most days were O.K., but some were really horrible, like the day Mrs. Evancich took Miranda and Terry to a horse show and I couldn't go. I was tired and lonely and the days were long. Chico was getting fat. Miranda called and begged me to play almost every day. How could I leave Mom? And how could I tell Mom how lonely I felt? I didn't want to worry her. So I didn't say a word.

One of the nice things was taking care of Trinidad. Some mornings he would wake up from his nap before Mom got home from seeing Father Tom. I would mix him a bottle of formula with warm water and feed it to him. He sucked hard when he ate and made little snuffling, snorting, piggy noises. It made me laugh out loud to hear him, and then he would jump because I had startled him. I tried hard not to laugh, but sometimes he was very funny. He always looked right at me and reached for my face with his tiny hands. Sometimes I let him grab my nose. I guess it was the first time I ever paid attention to a baby, and it made me think a lot more about our baby.

Mom was getting bigger and bigger. I wondered if the baby inside her was a boy or a girl. I wondered if it would like falling asleep in my arms like Trinidad did. I wondered if it would smell good and have soft, soft cheeks and hair. Then I'd think about Mom being so old and what happens when old moms have babies, and I wouldn't want to think about our baby anymore.

When the day came for Dad to come home from the hospital, my stomach had that frog feeling. Part of me wanted to see Dad so badly I could hardly stand waiting. Part of me wished he would stay in the hospital forever. Feeling both things at once mixed me up, made me feel mad at myself. What kind of kid doesn't want to see her own dad?

Mr. Abrigo came to pick up Mom and take her downtown to the hospital. I waved at them as the car pulled away. I was holding Trinidad and waved his little hand too.

About an hour later I heard Mr. Abrigo's car in the driveway. Marissa and Glendon were napping, and Trinidad had just fallen asleep in my arms. I was rocking him in the rocking chair. I didn't get up. I didn't want Trinidad to wake up. He was warm and soft and solid in my arms. And I felt scared about seeing Dad. It's hard to explain.

I heard Mr. Abrigo say, "Call me if you need anything," and then the kitchen door opened.

"Trina?" said Mom. "We're home." I took a deep breath and stood up. Trinidad didn't wake up. I thought about putting him in the bassinet we keep in the living room but decided to hold him instead. He was so peaceful. Dad hadn't seen him yet. I took a deep breath and walked out into the kitchen.

"Hi, Trina," said Dad. He looked skinnier and kind of pale, but he smiled at me, and his eyes looked more like himself than they had for a long, long time. "I missed you, Princess."

"I missed you too, Dad," I said, and my voice squeaked

and my eyes burned and all of a sudden I was crying and Dad was hugging me and Trinidad was squawking about being squeezed between us. Mom put her arms around all of us and we hugged for a long, long time.

THE next few weeks were pretty good. Dad seemed more like his old self, even though his shoulders drooped more than ever. His back hurt all the time, at least I think it did, because his eyes looked like he hurt. At first, right after he came home, he took only one short nap every day when it was extra hot. The rest of the time he kept busy. He worked in the garden, milked Priscilla, and reminded me when it was my turn to clean the barn. He helped Mom with the kids, so I had more time to ride Chico and hang around with Miranda. We rode and raced and visited the camp. We taught Goofy to fetch pop cans. And I thought about Dad a lot.

Dad didn't say anything about his stay at the hospital. Neither did Mom. I was dying to ask questions, but since neither of them said anything I didn't feel that I could either. We all pretended that nothing had happened, like those three weeks without Dad were just some sort of dream. Sometimes I felt like screaming at them to tell me the truth, but I was scared of what the truth might be. Pretending was a lot easier.

On the Fourth of July we went to the ocean for the day. The Abrigos took us all in their van. For once it didn't rain.

Mom and Dad and I walked along the shore for hours while Mrs. Abrigo read a spy book and got a tan and Mr. Abrigo slept on a blanket. We held hands most of the time, me between Dad and Mom, the three of us walking slowly along the hard, gray beach, walking slowly toward Oregon and California and Mexico and the Panama Canal and the South Pole. I looked for sand dollars and found one big, smooth, white one without any cracks. I found a seagull feather and a crab shell too. The shell stank. I threw it down and watched the waves pull it slowly into the water.

Dad told me and Mom the story about the time he went deep-sea fishing, how he'd spent the whole time barfing over the side while the other guys caught millions of fish. The way he told it was extra funny, because he never actually said *barf* or *throw up*; he just talked about it, and you knew exactly what he meant. He rolled his eyes and held his stomach, and I could picture him leaning over the side of the boat while everyone else pulled in the fish. The first salmon the other fishermen caught weighed fifty pounds. The second one weighed a hundred and fifty. Mom and I doubled over laughing at the huge, unbelievable fish and poor, sick, skinny Dad.

Dad didn't laugh; he just talked on and on in that low, quiet way of his. He didn't even crack a grin, but his blue eyes twinkled. It made the story that much funnier. We'd heard it before, every time we'd ever been to the ocean. He always told it in the same way, like it was the tragedy of his life to be sick and not catch fish. This time was the funniest and the best of all.

Wispy clouds flew past above the giant, smashing waves, and the sky was as blue as Dad's eyes. We were a family—laughing, holding hands, and being together without any bad feelings, or at least without thinking about the ones that were hiding down deep. I felt so good that I wished I could steal a pair of seagulls' wings and soar above the beach, dip between the waves, screech with the kind of happiness that makes you want to pop. I wanted that moment to go on and on. I wanted to stay there between my mom and dad and never let them go, to be twelve years old forever. It was that kind of a day.

When we got back Dad and Mr. Abrigo made a fire, and we roasted hot dogs on unbent coat hangers. Then we walked to the Indian-reservation fireworks stand and bought a bunch of good fireworks, the dangerous kind you can't buy in the city, like firecrackers, bottle rockets, sparklers, Piccolo Petes. It takes forever for night to come in July, so we roasted marshmallows and sang "John Jacob Jingleheimer Schmidt" about a million times. It made me think about YMCA camp, only five weeks away. Even Mrs. Abrigo sang. I sang really loud. I wondered if the baby could hear my voice.

Finally it got dark enough for fireworks. We went down to the beach. Mrs. Abrigo, who was pretty sunburned, brought a beach chair. The rest of us found driftwood logs to sit on. The moon was over the water and shone on the waves breaking against the dark flat beach. Somehow the waves seemed quieter, like they knew it was night. Dad took out some matches, and we lit fireworks on the sand until they were all gone. Mom and Mrs. Abrigo only wanted to do sparklers. Dad and Mr. Abrigo and I did all the rest.

We left just after the fireworks. Mr. Abrigo drove straight home except for a coffee stop at McDonald's. I went to the bathroom and discovered I'd started my period again. I'd skipped in June but I was ready. When we got back in the car I whispered it to Mom. She patted my leg, like I was her friend, not her kid. And for one second I didn't feel like a kid anymore. I decided I would tell Miranda next time we went to our camp.

We got home about one in the morning. I think about that Fourth of July a lot. It was one of the best days of my life. It was also the last happy time we had together as a family.

A few days after that Dad found out about Mom going to see Father Tom. He almost blew his stack. His eyes got big and his face turned red, and after all those weeks of no yelling I was sure he was going to scream. He didn't get all the way mad, but he got pretty close.

It was breakfast time, and Mom asked Dad if he'd like to go with her to see Father Tom sometime. "I told you, Anita. I don't go to church anymore." His words were tight, fast.

"We just talk," said Mom, not looking up from her bowl of cereal. "I thought you might like to come along."

"Talk about what?" Dad demanded.

"Oh, things on my mind," said Mom.

"If you've got problems, you tell them to *me*," yelled Dad. Then he made himself stop yelling. I could tell, because his cheeks twisted around and his mouth puckered. "Don't go spreading things about this family to that priest."

He said *priest* like a dirty word. *Father Tom was your friend,* I wanted to yell. *You used to play chess with him. Why did you stop? Why are you so mad at Father Tom?*

Dad hurt his back and lost his job. The calf was born crippled. Now Dad was taking medicine and seeing more doctors and Mom was expecting a baby and we never had enough money. But those things weren't Father Tom's fault. They couldn't be.

So whose fault were they? Were they God's fault? Does God care about things like jobs and babies when he has all those important things to take care of? I didn't know the answer. I wondered if that was what Dad thought, that it was God's fault that bad things had happened.

All of a sudden I knew why we quit going to church. Dad was mad at God.

I've been mad at God. The time Mom lost the other baby and I quit saying my prayers. I didn't want Dad to blame Father Tom. It wasn't fair. But at least I understood a little how he felt.

Mom didn't go back to Father Tom. One time when she was visiting the Abrigos I ran over to ask her something, and she and Mrs. Abrigo were sitting together in the window with their heads bowed, like maybe they were praying right there in the living room. Mrs. Abrigo had her arm around Mom. I went away without knocking. When Mom came back her eyes were red.

At first Dad took the bus downtown once a week to visit the doctor. He wasn't seeing our regular doctor, Dr. McKinley. Mom said he was seeing a special doctor. There wasn't anything wrong with Dad's body besides his bad back, she said. Even though she didn't say it out loud, I knew what she meant. Why couldn't she just say it? Why did she have to treat me like such a kid? I knew Dad was seeing a psychiatrist. I'm not stupid. I wanted to ask if that meant he was going crazy, but I was too scared to say it. By the end of July he was sleeping twice a day again. He missed his doctor's appointment two weeks in a row. Other than that he seemed O.K. He didn't yell. That's all I cared about.

It was the second week of August, and YMCA camp was only a few days away. The days were so hot and long that Miranda and I decided to build a real fort at our camp to pass the time more quickly. The blackberry vines were leafy and growing like crazy, crowding out the grassy space where we always liked to sit. The long, thorny vines hung down, and if they even touched us we got scratched. So we found some old boards and put up a wall, nailing the boards to the trees in a crooked rectangle.

We found one big board for the floor and laid it over the grass. Miranda's dad had made a greenhouse a few years ago, so she brought a piece of that wavy fiberglass stuff that lets light in. We put it on top for the roof.

It took us two days to get it all done. Mom didn't ask for any help at home. When we were finally finished with the fort, we brought a juice cooler full of red Kool-Aid and sandwiches and had a celebration. We tied the horses in the shade and crawled into our fort. I missed sitting in the grass, but at least the bugs wouldn't bite my legs so much. We sat on the board that was the floor, and Miranda spread out a picnic cloth she had brought along. I was supposed to bring the cups, but I forgot, so we took turns holding the jug up so the other person could drink out of the little spout. Miranda started giggling and spit red juice all over me. I got some in my mouth and spit it back at her, and we laughed so hard with juice all over us that I thought I'd wet my pants. Pretty soon we were sticky and sweaty and my stomach hurt from laughing.

It was a hot day, hot and still and heavy. Our fort had lots of holes, but there wasn't so much as a whisper of a breeze. The fiberglass roof let in light, but the trees above shaded us from the worst of the sun, so it was pretty cool inside. Miranda flopped onto her back and so did I. We sang "Kumbaya" and cracked up. Then for a while neither of us said anything. Finally Miranda spoke up.

"Are you packed?"

"No," I said. "It's still two days away."

"I'm already packed. Mom bought me a new swimsuit."

"I'm not packing until the night before," I said, "in case I need something." A fly buzzed lazily around my head. I closed my eyes and thought about floating around the camp lake in a canoe. There would probably be a lot of mosquitoes. It would be worth it. I'd never been in a canoe.

"How's your Dad?" asked Miranda.

"Fine," I said, but I didn't look at her when I said it.

"Your mom is getting really fat."

"She's eight months along," I said. "She's starting to decorate the extra bedroom. I had to help paint."

"What do you think it feels like to be pregnant?" asked

Miranda. She sat up, wadded the picnic cloth into a ball, and stuck it under her T-shirt. "How do I look?"

"Stupid," I said. "Here, let me try it." Miranda pulled out the picnic cloth and gave it to me. I stuffed it under my T-shirt.

"You look just like your mom."

"Except for my boobs. Mom's are huge now." I patted the T-shirt baby.

"At least you have some," said Miranda, and pulled her T-shirt tight across her chest. "You flat pancakes!" she yelled. She beat her flat chest with both fists. "Swell!" I pulled the picnic-cloth baby out and threw it at her head. Miranda acted like it knocked her over. She lay on the floor with her feet against one wall. "Nothing works," she said with a giggle. "Those green M&M's were a total waste. Guess I'll just have to wait."

"It won't be long," I said. "Guess what? I started."

"No way!" Miranda sat up. She stared at me like I was some kind of swamp creature. "When?"

"A while back."

"What is it like?" asked Miranda. "How much blood comes out? Did you try tampons? Do you get cramps that make you want to die?" Her questions really embarrassed me a lot.

"It's not that big a deal," I said. "You'll find out soon enough yourself."

"Are you kidding? My mom didn't start her period until she was fourteen!" Miranda flicked a beetle off her shoe. "I can't believe you didn't tell me the first time."

"I was embarrassed," I said. And I didn't want everyone else to know. I didn't care so much now.

"I'm going to tell *everyone* when I start," said Miranda, and I knew she wasn't kidding.

"Did you get your list of classes?" I asked.

"Yesterday. They came in the mail."

"Who'd you get?"

"Sternich for home room, Meyers for math—"

"I got Meyers too," I said.

"Second period?" she asked. I nodded. "Oh, good!" Miranda clapped and stamped her feet against the side of the fort. "After that I got Renchek for English. She looks like a pelican." We giggled and I told her I had Renchek too, only not until fifth period.

"Does she really look like a pelican?" I asked.

"Terry says she has this incredible nose like a beak and flubbery skin that hangs down from her neck. They call her Mrs. Pelican behind her back."

"That's mean," I said.

"Just wait," said Miranda. "You'll die laughing when you see her."

"It's still mean." I promised myself I wouldn't laugh when I saw Mrs. Renchek for the first time.

"I have first lunch," said Miranda. "What did you get?"

"Second." I'd been hoping we'd at least have the same lunch.

"Oh, no!" wailed Miranda. "What am I going to do at lunchtime?"

"*Duuhh*," I said. "Eat lunch." Miranda giggled. She'd find

plenty to do. In a couple of days she'd have sixteen new friends. That's just the way she is. Friends take longer for me.

"After lunch I have science," said Miranda. "I forget the teacher's name. Something Polish and hard." I kicked her. "Oh, sorry, *sorry!*" she said, rubbing her leg. "Polish and easy and very elegant." We both cracked up.

"I have art after science," said Miranda.

"I don't have art this semester," I said. "I have home ec."

"Home yeck, you mean," said Miranda, sticking out her tongue. "Do you have Hobson? I heard she pokes you with a straight pin if you talk in class."

"No way!" I had Hobson. Room 2.

"No lie." Miranda turned on her side and propped her head up with one arm. "Terry had her last year. He hated her. Do you have geography?"

"Third period. After that I have P.E."

"I have P.E. last."

The fly buzzed against one of the boards. I heard one of the horses snort and stomp outside. Only one class together and it was math, so we wouldn't get to talk at all. We wouldn't even have the same lunch. And no recesses.

"It sure is going to be different at Lincoln," said Miranda. "Different from grade school." She flicked another little black beetle with one finger.

"There'll be way more kids," I said.

"And tons more homework," said Miranda. The fly landed on a red punch spot on the board floor. I shooed it away with my foot.

"I heard the ninth graders throw nickels and dimes on

the floor just to see if the seventh graders will pick them up," I said. "If you pick one up they call you a scrounge forever."

"Do you think it's true?" asked Miranda. "Do you think they really throw money? Do you think they ever throw quarters? Quarters would be worth it."

"I didn't hear anything about quarters," I said. I tried to imagine the long hallways littered with shiny coins and the big kids just waiting to laugh and call us names. They wouldn't catch me, not even with quarters.

"Do you think your mom will make you baby-sit a lot?" asked Miranda.

"I don't know. When our baby comes that'll be five little kids, at least in the afternoons. Wayne is starting kindergarten."

The fly came back with a friend. They found the sticky red spot and landed. Miranda took a deep breath and whispered the thing I'd wanted to say ever since we'd started talking about seventh grade.

"I hope we still have time to ride, Trina, at least once in a while."

"Me too." I reached over and squeezed Miranda's hand. She squeezed back. For a while we just stared up at the tree shadows dancing on the fiberglass roof, holding hands, thinking about seventh grade and all the things that were going to change. Outside Chico whinnied. There was a thump and a squeal and another thump, and then it was quiet again.

"Somebody must have his nose up somebody else's behind," said Miranda with a wide, mischievous grin. "Race you home!" She grabbed the juice jug and the picnic cloth and charged out of the fort. I crumpled up the paper bags and ran after her. We jumped on the horses and raced all the way to Miranda's house.

Chico and I won by a nose.

WHEN I got home I was a sweaty, smelly, sticky mess. I brushed Chico down and filled the water trough for him. Priscilla came trotting up from the pasture for a drink too. I scratched her between the ears and swished away the flies around her eyes.

The day-care kids were playing in the sandbox. Marissa was filling up her pants with sand, Wayne was digging canals with a stick, and Glendon was pouring sand in his hair and rubbing it in like shampoo. I went inside to take a shower.

It was cooler in the house but not much. I found Mom rocking Trinidad and giving him his bottle. All he had on was a diaper. Mom wiped her damp, straggly hair out of her face with one hand, waved at me and smiled and then put her fingers to her lips so I wouldn't make noise. Dad was asleep on the couch.

He'd been sleeping a lot for the last couple of weeks, most of the day, in fact. I tried not to worry about it. I told myself his back probably hurt from all the gardening. And it *was* the hottest part of the summer. I waved back at Mom and tiptoed upstairs.

After showering and changing my clothes, I went back downstairs. Mom was still in the rocking chair. She had put

Trinidad in the bassinet and was resting with her eyes shut. She was tired all the time now, and taking care of four extra kids didn't help. I stood in the doorway and watched her sleep. She looked peaceful. Her face was relaxed enough for the wrinkles not to show too much. It made her look a lot younger, like Mrs. Evancich. I was just about to look for something to eat when Mom gasped and her eyes opened wide. She held her breath and closed her eyes again, but now her face was full of pain.

"Mom!" I cried, and hurried to the rocking chair. "Are you okay?" She nodded a couple of times but didn't open her eyes. She was still holding her breath. Finally she let it out with a *whoosh*. There were little beads of sweat on her forehead and across her upper lip.

"What's wrong?" I asked.

"Don't talk so loud," said Mom, and nodded toward where Dad was snoring on the couch.

"Okay, okay," I said in a whisper. "Why did you look like that? Did the baby kick really hard?" Mom didn't answer. She heaved herself out of the chair, and I followed her out into the kitchen.

"Would you get me a drink, Trina?" I filled a glass with ice and water from the fridge. Mom sat down at the table. I gave her the water and watched her drink it. She wiped the sweat off her face with one hand.

"I've been having contractions off and on all day."

"But it's a whole month early!" I said. I looked at Mom's swollen belly. It looked the same to me, big and bulging with a kid that was my little brother or sister.

"It's probably just a false alarm," said Mom. "That's why I haven't said anything." She sighed and ran finger through the wet ring on the tabletop. "I didn't want to worry your dad."

"Maybe you should see the doctor," I said. My heart was racing. I watched Mom's belly for signs of . . . what? Weren't some babies born at home because the moms didn't make it to the doctor in time? How would a kid like me know what to do? *"Please* go to the doctor, Mom. This is serious." I tried to sound grown-up. I wanted her to listen to me, to go to the doctor. I didn't want that baby to be born at home.

"I guess I'd better," said Mom with a sigh. "They'll probably check me and send me home. That happened with you, you know." I remembered Mom's story of false labor, how Dad had raced her to the hospital in the middle of the night only to be sent home to wait another week until I was born. Babies were unpredictable. I knew that much.

"I'll wake up Dad," I said.

"Please, Trina," she said, grabbing my hand. "He's been so tired lately. Don't bother him."

"But Dad should know," I said.

"Let's wait until we're positive," said Mom. "No need to bother him yet, not for a silly false alarm." She closed her eyes and bit her lower lip. She squeezed my hand so hard it hurt. When she started breathing again she was panting, like she'd run a long, long way. I grabbed the phone and dialed the Abrigos' phone number. Mom didn't try to stop me.

Five minutes later I heard the familiar sound of the

Abrigos' van pulling into our driveway. Mr. Abrigo helped Mom into the car. Mrs. Abrigo put her arm around my shoulder and squished me against her soft, fat body. She smelled of bread dough and fruity perfume. I waved at Mom as Mr. Abrigo pulled the van out of the driveway, but she didn't see me. Her eyes were shut again.

The day-care kids came tromping in from the sandbox right after that. Mrs. Abrigo and I cleaned them up and fixed snacks. I changed Trinidad's diaper and put him in the baby swing. Wayne got down from the table and started whining about being too hot. Mrs. Abrigo told me to put on the sprinkler and let the kids run under the spray. I was on my way out to the yard to hook up the hose when the phone rang.

"Somebody answer the damn phone!"

Dad. I'd forgotten all about him. I ran to the phone and picked up the receiver before it could ring a second time.

"Hello?"

"Mr. Stenkawsky, please." I put my hand over the mouthpiece.

"Dad! It's for you."

"I'm resting," yelled Dad. "Take a message." I sighed and took my hand away.

"May I take a message?" I asked the phone.

"My name is Doctor Yamori. I'm calling about Mrs. Anita Stenkawsky."

"Is she okay?" I cried. Mrs. Abrigo came over and stood next to me.

"She's fine," said the voice. "She just delivered a baby."

"A *baby!*" I started screaming. "A baby, a baby, a baby!"
Mrs. Abrigo took the phone away from me. "Dad, Mom had
the baby!"

I ran into the living room. My dad was sitting on the
edge of the couch. His hair was a mess and his eyes were
puffy and swollen from sleep. In the corner of his mouth
there was some dry white stuff, like he'd drooled or something. He tucked in his shirt and looked right through me,
like I wasn't even there.

"Dad," I said. "Mom just had the baby." He looked up at
me and blinked. Then he got off the couch in slow motion.
His eyes, those puffy, sleepy eyes, never left my face. His
bushy gray eyebrows came together in a frown and his face
turned beet red. When he was standing all the way up he
grabbed my shoulders hard and shook me.

"Why didn't someone tell me?" He shouted in my face.
"How come you let me sleep through it?" His breath was
horrible, like something dead. "Why did you let me sleep,
Trina?"

"Mom said it was a false alarm," I said. My voice was like
a mouse voice, squeaky and little. "She just went for
a check."

"And she didn't think I'd want to know?" His eyes were
bulging. His fingers dug into my shoulders like spikes. Spit
came out and hit me in the face. I was scared, so scared I felt
a little pee warm my underpants. I squeezed my legs
together.

"She told me not to wake you up," I cried. "It was just a

false alarm." Out of the corner of my eye I saw Mrs. Abrigo in the doorway.

"Mitch," said Mrs. Abrigo, but my Dad didn't hear her. He pushed me away and brushed past her. I heard the back door slam.

I didn't start to cry until Mrs. Abrigo came and put her arms around me. We sank down on the couch together hugging like that, and for once I didn't mind her fruity smell.

"I don't understand," I cried. "I try so hard not to make him mad. He didn't used to be mad all the time, not before, not before." I sobbed and blubbered, and Mrs. Abrigo went *shh, shh, shh.*

The three day-care kids stood in the doorway and stared. "Find something on the TV, Wayne, honey," said Mrs. Abrigo. "Trina's daddy's a little crabby. He'll feel better later."

I heard the television switch on and then the sound of a cereal commercial. My nose was running and I kept sniffling until Mrs. Abrigo reached into her pocket and pulled out a clean tissue. "Here," she said. "Use this." I wiped my nose. "It's a girl," whispered Mrs. Abrigo.

"A girl?" All of a sudden I remembered the baby. I was a sister. I had a little sister. "Is the baby, my sister, is she okay?" Mrs. Abrigo frowned.

"Well, that doctor, he said she's kinda early and they were all keeping an eye on her."

"Was there anything wrong with her?" *Is she retarded?* I was dying to ask.

"I don't think so," said Mrs. Abrigo. "Just early." A car pulled into the driveway. "I bet that's Joe." Mrs. Abrigo stood up and hurried to the kitchen.

"Hey, hey, hey!" said Mr. Abrigo as he came through the door. "How's the big sister doin'?" He tweaked my nose and flopped down into one of the kitchen chairs. He told us how Mom's contractions had gotten really close and hard and how by the time they got to the hospital she couldn't even walk.

"They wheeled her away and I'm not kiddin', five minutes later, okay, maybe ten, out comes this doctor askin' am I Mr. Stenkawsky!" He took a drink of the water that Mrs. Abrigo had set down on the table. She had Trinidad under one arm. "So anyhow, I tell the doctor no, but I'm the guy that brought her in, and he says it's a girl! Yours never came so fast, Angie, did they?"

"Nope. Tony was the fastest. Five hours." Mrs. Abrigo took Trinidad's fist out of his mouth and put in a pacifier.

"I thought it was Jimmy," said Mr. Abrigo.

"No, it was Tony. I oughta know, Joe."

"How's my mom?" I asked. "Did you see her?"

"Ya mean after?" said Mr. Abrigo. I nodded.

"No, I came straight here." He took another drink of water. "To get your dad and you. I'm sure she's just fine. Where's Mitch, anyhow?"

"He got kinda jumpy when Trina here told him the news," said Mrs. Abrigo. "He went out the back door. We haven't seem him since."

"Nerves," said Mr. Abrigo with a wink. "New dads are always nervous. I'll go see if he's in the garden," he said, and went out the back door. I took Trinidad from Mrs. Abrigo and jiggled him on my lap. When Mr. Abrigo came back into the house he had a puzzled look on his face.

"I looked all over the place," he said. "Can't figure out where he got to." He scratched his head. "Well, come on, Trina. Let's go take a look at that new baby."

I told them I had to go to the bathroom and ran up to change my underwear. I shut my eyes tight, really tight, trying to get the picture out of my mind of Dad yelling and his eyes bulging because I hadn't told him that Mom went to the hospital. She only went for a check! It wasn't my fault the baby came so fast. We didn't know. *We didn't know!*

And besides, if he cared so much about Mom and the baby, why wasn't he here with us now getting ready to go see her? Why didn't he ask how she was or how the baby was? He'd just been mad, boiling, popping mad. He didn't even ask if it was a boy or a girl. When I thought about it that way, it made me mad, mad at my dad. Why did he have to act so crazy?

Mrs. Abrigo stayed with the day-care kids. She waved at us from the kitchen door and said to give Mom a hug from her.

"Things are real different now," said Mr. Abrigo. "Our first two kids were born at home, in Italy. The rest were born here, in the hospital, like good Americans." He talked and talked, remembering each child's birth, how long it took, how small the babies were, how fast they'd grown up. "And now they're having babies themselves," he said. "I got sixteen grandkids, Trina."

This was not news to me. Pictures of the Abrigos' sixteen grandchildren were plastered all over the walls of their house along with pictures of the Virgin Mary and Saint Francis and a big sad-eyed plastic Jesus on the cross. I let him talk without listening. A sister! What would she be like? What would Mom and Dad name her?

"Dads nowadays gotta be in there with the mother," said Mr. Abrigo. He shook his head. "Not me, no way. When Angie was havin' babies, that was women's stuff. They didn't let the dads get anywhere near the delivery room. And those Italian midwives were even worse! Wouldn't even let us in the house!"

"Here we are, Princess," said Mr. Abrigo. "Good old Saint Teri's. Four of my kids were born here. Back then all the nurses were nuns, but not anymore." He pulled up to the main entrance. "Hop out while I find a place to park. Meet you upstairs in the maternity ward. OB they call it nowadays. Room 304."

I got out in front of the main entrance to Saint Theresa's Hospital. The stone steps led up to the big, wide doors with carved angels above and a NO SMOKING sign off to one side. I'd been up those stairs a lot when Dad hurt his back. We'd visited almost every day. Mom and I had raced up the stairs, two at a time, to see who could get to the top first. I hurried up again this time.

The nurse at the desk was small and tidy-looking. She wore her glasses on the end of her nose, like a cartoon of a schoolteacher. When I told her who I was she smiled and pointed down the long, shiny corridor toward Mom's room. It was hard not to run.

At first I thought Mom was asleep. She was lying on her bed with her eyes shut. Her face was pale, and there were big dark circles under her eyes. There was an IV dripping into one arm. But the biggest thing I noticed was how skinny she looked. She looked exactly like a popped balloon, and the thought of it made me giggle. Mom opened her eyes and smiled. "Hi, Trina Jean," she said.

"Hi, Mom." All of a sudden I felt shy. She reached one hand toward me, the one with the IV taped to it. I took her hand. It felt cold. "How are you feeling?"

"Pooped," she said. "The doctor says I'll have to stay a few extra days, until I get my strength back. I'm too old to be having babies." I nodded. Maybe she'd worried about that too.

"How's the baby?" I asked.

"She's doing fine, for being a month early. She's pretty small, only four and a half pounds. They put her in a special part of the nursery."

"Is she . . . is she . . . " The words were stuck but I had to ask. I took a deep breath. "Is she normal?" There. I had said it. The words were out and now I'd know for sure. I bit my lower lip and waited.

"Normal?" Mom frowned. "She looked normal to me. Nobody said anything to me about her not being normal. She's just tiny."

I hugged my mom hard, being careful not to get tangled up in the IV tube. I felt silly for worrying that the baby would be retarded. I was glad I'd never told Mom what Miranda had said. "Can I see her? Can I see her right now?"

"Sure. Go ask the nurse to show you where the babies are." Mom pushed a strand of hair behind my ear. "I'm so glad you're happy, Trina," she said. Her smile was tired but her eyes sparkled at me, and I knew she wasn't faking it.

"I *am* happy, Mom," I said, and skipped all the way down the hall to find my sister.

The babies were in two rooms. One room had little clear plastic cribs on top of carts with wheels. The boy babies had blue cards taped to their cribs and the girl babies had pink cards. The cards had names. Roberta Marie Rozzi. William John Kaplan. Shannon Deborah Erickson. Evan Malcom James-Appleby, Jr. A lot of people stood outside the big window, reading the names on the cards, looking for that one special baby they had come to see for the first time. Without those name cards it would have been pretty crazy. The babies looked a lot alike to me.

The other room had incubators. There were three babies in incubators and two nurses all dressed in green gowns and face masks. One of them saw me standing in the door. He dropped the mask from around his mouth and asked me if he could help me. I said I was Trina Stenkawsky, that I wanted to see my little sister. He gave me a gown and a face mask, and I went into the incubator room with him.

"Your sister is fine," he said. "She's just a little small. We have to make sure she keeps warm and is eating well. Then she can go home."

"How long will that be?" I asked, looking at the babies.

"At least a week or two," said the nurse.

"Which one is she?" I asked through my mask.

"That one." He pointed to the farthest incubator. I walked over and peeked in. There, on a soft piece of sheepskin lay my sister. I touched the glass, wanting to feel her. She was like a doll, only more perfect, more soft-looking, and more beautiful. Her skin was pink. She had a lot of red hair too—tons! All she had on was a tiny diaper, and I could see her bulgy belly button where the cord was still clamped. It was bigger than I thought.

"Do you want to touch her?" asked the other nurse. She came over and stood by me. She was big and smiley and smelled of soap. I nodded. "Well then, wash your hands with that pink goop over there." She pointed to the sink and a bottle of liquid soap. I washed fast and hard.

"All right now, honey," said the nurse. "You just put your hands through these little holes." It was warm inside. I reached down and touched my sister's miniature fingers.

"She has fingernails!" I said, and both nurses laughed. I put my finger in my sister's hand, and she grabbed it hard. I didn't know babies were so strong! Then I petted her tummy and her foot and her hair. I touched my sister's cheek, and she turned her head toward me, her big, round eyes wide open. I know she saw me because she squinted and kind of frowned like she was trying hard to figure out what I was. I laughed. Then I saw the card. It was pink, like the ones taped to the other girl babies' cribs. It said BABY GIRL STENKAWSKY.

Baby Girl. I wondered what Mom and Dad were going to

name her. The other babies already had names. I couldn't remember Mom and Dad ever talking about names, but then they hadn't talked about the baby much at all when I was around. I thanked the nurses. They took my mask and gown, and I hurried back to talk to Mom.

Just before I got to Mom's door I stopped cold. Dad was inside. I could hear his voice. I wanted to rush in, tell them I'd seen the baby, but I didn't want to see Dad, not after all that yelling. I waited outside the door for a minute, then I slowly peeked around the doorway.

Dad was on his knees beside Mom's bed. For a second I wondered if he'd fallen down. Then I heard him. He was crying. His shoulders shook and he sobbed into his arms on the bed beside Mom. It made the skin on the back of my arms prickle and made my stomach feel queasy to see him like that. I wanted to run away.

"I'm sorry, Anita," cried Dad. "What kind of a husband am I, anyhow? I should have been here with you. When Trina told me, I blew up at her. What kind of a dad is that? Will you ever forgive me?" Mom's eyes were shut, and the painful look on her face was back. The hand with the IV tube was petting Dad on the head, like he was a day-care kid.

Mom didn't say anything. Tears squeezed out of the corners of her closed eyes. She just kept petting Dad, and he kept sobbing and crying and saying what a terrible husband and father he was, how he took the bus as soon as he could, how we didn't deserve a jerk like him.

When your own dad is bawling it's the scariest thing in the world, even scarier than when he is really mad and shaking you. I leaned against the cool hallway wall and took a couple of deep breaths. My legs were shaking. I wanted to sit down. I couldn't go in, not with him in there, not with him crying and her petting him on the head. I just couldn't do it. I went downstairs and found Mr. Abrigo.

"Mom's tired now," I said. "Could we go home?"

"Sure, Princess," said Mr. Abrigo. He stood up and folded the paper he was reading. "Beats me where your dad ran off to. You'll have to tell him all about that little baby when he comes home."

I didn't tell him where Dad was. He would have made us wait. I couldn't stand the thought of waiting for Dad to come out, riding home in the car with him, sitting next to him while Mr. Abrigo told all his stories.

On the way home I heard about Uncle Luigi's liver cancer and how Grandma Abrigo had sixteen babies at home. I smiled and made all the right noises to act like I was listening. It was hard not to show what I really felt, how my insides were jumbled up and hurting, how my own dad was acting like some crazy stranger, how my mom was crying and shushing my dad like a baby on the one day she should have been happiest of all.

Baby Girl Stenkawsky. I thought about my new red-haired sister with the tiny fists and the eyes that squinted when she looked at me. I wondered how I would tell Miranda that I couldn't go to camp now, not with Mom and the baby in the hospital. I wondered how long it would be before my baby sister had a name.

WE named my sister on the day Miranda left for YMCA camp. I was sad about not going, but the baby seemed much more important, and Dad needed me at home. Even though Mom said I should still go, how could I? Miranda was totally disappointed, even when I gave my free-week certificate to her so she could bring another friend. She said she didn't *have* another friend, which is a lie, and gave the certificate to Terry. They promised to make me something in leather-craft class.

Mom and I chose my sister's name. Dad said the name didn't matter to him as long as we didn't choose Mildred. So I helped Mom decide by telling her which names I hated because they reminded me of kids at school. Mom picked Erin. I like Erin a lot. I don't know any other kid with that name. I chose Elaine because it's Miranda's middle name. Erin Elaine Stenkawsky. It's a name with a good sound.

I went to the hospital to see Mom and Erin every day. Mr. Abrigo took me the first couple of days. After that I took the bus. I liked the quietness of Saint Teri's. I even liked the smell. I also liked sitting next to Mom on the bed and watching the TV high on the wall. And I liked going with her to the nursery when it was time to feed Erin.

Erin was still too weak to suck well. It made her so tired that she fell asleep instead of finishing. So Mom had to hook up to this suction-cup thing called a breast pump. It made a lot of weird vacuum cleaner noises, and milk came out of Mom's breast, down a tube, and into a little plastic jar. Mom pumped both sides. A lot of milk came out.

After that the nurse would put the milk in a bottle the size of a doll's bottle. Then Mom would hold Erin in the rocking chair and feed her, squeezing a little milk in and letting her swallow it. She had to wear a gown and a mask. So did I.

Erin was bundled up in so many blankets that you could hardly see her, trying to suck up the milk. Sometimes she'd choke. The first time it freaked me out. She gagged and spit milk all over Mom. But it didn't bother Mom. She just talked low and quiet and patted Erin until she was done choking. Feeding Erin was a lot of work. It was hard to get her to stay awake long enough to drink even half of the little bottle. The nurses saved Mom's milk and fed Erin between the times Mom fed her. But it wasn't working. She wasn't gaining weight very well. After she was done eating I got to hold her. That was the best part.

After the first day Dad seemed a little better. I never told Mom I saw Dad crying, and she didn't mention it. We all pretended that nothing had happened. Dad didn't cry or yell at me anymore. He came with me to visit only once. We stopped by the nursery window and looked in at Erin. Dad said she looked a lot like I had looked. I asked if he wanted to hold her, but he said he was too nervous to hold such a small baby. He looked so sad and awful and tired that I wished he hadn't come. It was hard to forget how I'd seen him that first day, crying and sobbing beside Mom's hospital bed.

After we looked at Erin, Dad visited Mom for a while. He told her about the beets and the corn. He told her Priscilla was giving lots of milk. Then Dad said, "How's the baby?" and Mom said, "She's doing fine," but they didn't talk much.

I think Mom was afraid of worrying Dad. She hates it when other people worry. And maybe Dad still felt embarrassed about not being there when Erin was born and about crying. Everything was uncomfortable when he was there. It wasn't the way families should be when they have a new baby. I kept wishing he would go home and felt guilty for wishing it.

Dad didn't stay long enough to help feed Erin. I was glad when he got up to go. "Take care of Mom," he said. "She needs you." Then he was gone. I stayed with Mom and Erin until it was time to take the bus home. I held Erin four times and even helped change her diaper. She had the teeniest rear end you've ever seen.

When I was at home I tried hard to make sure everything was perfect for Dad. I milked Priscilla in the morning so he wouldn't have to get up early. I made his favorite breakfast the first couple of days, but he didn't get up in time to eat it. After that I just left the cereal boxes on the table before I went to see Mom. When I came home from the hospital I always tried to make something good for dinner. One night I heated chili and cut up chunks of cheese to go in it. Another night I made bacon-and-lettuce-and-tomato sandwiches. I don't know if it was my cooking or what, but Dad wasn't eating much. He hardly ate a thing, no matter what good stuff I tried to fix him. Most of the time he slept. At least he didn't yell at me or ask to visit Mom again.

I wondered if Dad felt a little left out, I mean, the mom and the baby are the main people at a time like this. I tried not to think too much about all his sleeping. At least when he was sleeping he wasn't upset. I did my best to keep him from getting mad, and I guess I did O.K., because he didn't seem to notice me much at all.

I thought a lot about Miranda at camp. I missed her, and I was sure Chico was going to get fat eating all that grass and not exercising. I just didn't feel that I could leave Dad home by himself if I didn't have to, even if all he did was sleep. And if the phone rang, if Mom called, I wanted to be right there to talk to her. Once when she called, Mom asked if Dad was taking his medicine. I said I didn't know. What I didn't tell her was that I was too scared to ask him.

It's a weird feeling to take care of your parents, but that's exactly what I did. For five whole days I was either at home or at the hospital or somewhere between the two. There wasn't much time left over for things like riding horses. It was probably better that Miranda was away. That way I didn't have to tell her I couldn't ride.

I didn't mind being at the hospital with Mom and Erin. Being at home was harder. I fixed food, washed dishes, fed Chico, cleaned the barn, read books, and waited for the next time I could visit Mom and Erin. I didn't bother Dad and he didn't bother me.

The day-care kids were gone. They wouldn't be back until Erin was home and Mom was ready for a full house again. The house was dead quiet without the kids. As much of a pain as they were, I missed them, even Wayne the whiner. Most of the time the only sounds in the whole house were Dad's snoring and the sound of my own heart. The house was empty. So was I.

The day Mom came home I was both happy and sad. Erin wasn't ready to come home. Her weight had dropped a little, which Mom said was normal for all babies at first, but she hadn't gained it back even with all the extra feeding. She had to weigh at least five pounds to come home, and she had to be eating well on her own. It was depressing news. It's no wonder Mom's shoulders drooped and her cheeks sagged and the breast pump in its little suitcase looked like it weighed a million pounds. I met her at the door.

"Where's Dad?" she asked, kissing me on the cheek.

"Sleeping," I said. She didn't tell me to wake him up and I didn't offer.

Mrs. Abrigo brought spaghetti and meatballs for dinner that night. Dad was still sleeping. Mom and I ate without him. "When can Erin come home?" I asked.

"Soon, I hope," said Mom. "Maybe in a week or so." Mom cut a meatball in half. She stabbed it with her fork but didn't put it in her mouth. "How has Dad been this week?"

"Okay, I guess." Was sleeping all day O.K.? It sure was better than yelling.

"Is he sleeping a lot?" She looked right at me when she asked that, and I knew what she wanted to hear. I had to tell her the truth.

"Yeah," I said, looking down at the noodles on my plate. "Most of the time." Mom sighed. She put down her fork and rested her head in both hands. "But he hasn't been mad or upset the whole time," I said. "And he's excited about the baby. He said he can't *wait* for her to come home." A lie. After his only visit to the hospital he never mentioned Erin. He hardly spoke at all. I hated seeing Mom like that, ignoring her dinner, looking a hundred years old.

"Trina, I'm really worried about Dad."

It was the tone of her voice that surprised me the most. It was like she was talking to another grown-up. Mom had never talked to me that way before. And Mom had never talked to me about Dad, except to say that his back hurt or that he was tired. There was something more to her words, something deeper than hurt backs or anything else.

I was worried about Dad too. So were the Abrigos. Otherwise why would they call every day and ask about him? We were all worried about Dad.

"This is hard for me to say, Trina," said Mom, "but you need to know. You need to know in case—" She didn't finish. I knew what she was going to say. A glob of food stuck in my throat. *In case he's going crazy.*

"Do you remember the night Dad went to the hospital?" asked Mom. I nodded. I would remember that night forever. "Do you know why he had to be in the hospital?"

"You said he needed peace and quiet. You said he had a

nervous breakdown." Mom looked up. She looked me right in the eye, and in that very second she looked at me exactly like one grown-up looks at another. It scared me like crazy. She took a deep breath.

"Dad threatened to kill himself."

"Dad?" The word barely escaped my lips. *No way.*

Mom nodded, still looking at me in that grown-up way. "I had him admitted to the hospital. He wasn't very happy about it. He refused to see me the whole time."

"Why didn't you tell me?" My eyes filled with tears. Mom was a blur.

"I wanted to protect you, Trina," said Mom. "It's an awful burden for a child to carry. I didn't want you to worry."

Suddenly it all fitted together, everything over the last year and a half, Dad hurting his back, losing his job, sleeping more and more, all the yelling and the furious, crazy, desperate looks, his sad, empty eyes. And then he had lost the calf, the calf that was going to make us some money. And Mom was pregnant and we needed money and Mrs. Evancich bought me the expensive dress and then, the night of the dance, Dad said he wanted to—I couldn't even think the words.

For more than a year we'd tried so hard, both of us, me and Mom, tried so hard all the time not to upset Dad, tried not to spend money, tried to be quiet, tried to make sure everything went just right for him, tried not to wake the sleeping monster that lived inside him. Now I knew what that monster was.

"I thought he was upset about the baby," I said. I didn't

tell her how worried *I'd* been or why. I'll never tell her that. "I thought he didn't want Erin."

"Dad is too sick to know what he wants."

That was it, really. Dad was sick. Sick, sick, sick. Just then I heard him snore in the other room. Here we were talking about him like he wasn't even home. In a way he wasn't. He hadn't been for a long time.

"He was better after the hospital," I said.

"For a while," admitted Mom. "But I'm pretty sure he's stopped taking the medicine they gave him."

"But *why?*" I cried.

"I don't know, Trina. I don't know."

"Then we have to *make* him take it!" I said. "Please, Mom, make him take it." Mom sighed and shook her head.

"Don't you think I've tried?" Tears spilled down her cheeks. She reached across the table and held my hand. "Your father is a grown man. I can only do so much. I can't *make* him get well, don't you see? Don't you think if there was anything more I could do for Dad I would?"

She looked at me through her tears, straight at me, straight through me, and for a second she wasn't sad or tired or worried. She was strong. "I've got myself and you and Erin to worry about."

"So what are we going to do?" I asked. *What now?* I thought about telling Mom to sneak Dad's medicine into his food, but I knew that she would never do it.

"I'll try to talk to him tomorrow," she said. She sighed and rubbed the back of her neck. "I'll do what I can."

We finished our supper without talking. There were so

many thoughts going through my head that I couldn't even put them into sentences. It was like a gigantic flood of words, feelings of being scared and mixed up and worried. I felt I couldn't breathe. I felt like I was drowning.

I knew. I knew what was wrong with Dad. And it was worse than going crazy.

I did all the dishes and cleaned up the kitchen. Miranda called to tell me all about camp. I don't remember much of it, only that the pancakes were like Frisbees. All I could think about was Dad. Miranda asked if I wanted to go shopping for school supplies the next day. I said I couldn't but thanked her for asking. I could tell by her voice she was disappointed. How could I tell her I had more important things on my mind than notebooks and pencils? How could a kid from a perfect family like hers ever understand how I felt?

After I hung up the phone I headed upstairs to bed. Mom was already in her room. "Good night," I called in to her.

"Good night, Trina Jean," she said, and then I heard a click and the breast-pump motor started up.

I must have fallen asleep right away, because the next thing I remember was the sun peeking through my curtains and Dad yelling downstairs. His voice made my heart thump and my mouth dry up. I listened hard, but I couldn't hear his words. I couldn't hear Mom's words either, but I could hear her voice. She was reasoning and convincing and begging, the way she gets Marissa to take her medicine. Dad talked and Mom talked. I could hardly breathe. I heard the back door slam shut.

I lay in bed for another half hour, just to be sure that Dad wasn't around. I didn't want to see him at all, knowing what I knew. I wondered what Mom was doing. When I finally went downstairs she was sitting at the kitchen table drinking a cup of coffee. She smiled when she saw me.

"I forgot all about school, Trina," she said. "How many more days until classes start?"

"School starts on Monday," I said. I poured myself some cereal. Dad's coffee cup was full. He hadn't touched it.

"How much money do you need for school supplies?"

"I don't need anything, Mom," I said. "I've got pencils and stuff from last year."

"Don't be silly," said Mom. She reached for her purse on

the back of her chair, opened it, and dug through her wallet. She handed me ten dollars. "Why don't you call Miranda and see if she wants to go shopping? Time's running out."

"Don't we need this money?" The ten-dollar bill was crisp and smooth in my hand.

"Yes," said Mom. "We need it for you to buy school supplies." She finished her coffee and stood up. She crossed to where I was sitting and put her hand on my cheek. "Go on. Call Miranda. I know she loves to shop." She smiled and tweaked my nose. "Besides, I've got an appointment with that awful breast pump, and then I'm going down to the hospital to be with Erin. You've been home enough lately."

"What about Dad?" I finally asked.

"He'll be fine," said Mom. "We had a talk." *It sounded like a fight to me*, I thought, but I didn't say it. "Dad promised to take his medicine and see the doctor tomorrow."

"Do you think he'll do it?" I bit the inside of my cheek while I waited for her to answer.

"I hope so, Trina."

Mom looked at me in that same grown-up way. I stared into her eyes, searching them for the answer that I wanted so badly. *Say yes, Mom. Say he's going to get better.* But she didn't know any more than I did what Dad was going to do for sure. How can one person say what another one will do? There is just no way to know.

I stood up and put my arms around Mom. I hugged her hard for a long time, and pretty soon she was rocking me from side to side, like she does with a baby. It felt good to squeeze and hold my mom like that. It felt good to be rocked. It didn't make me feel like a baby at all. It made me feel safe. It made me hope for good things.

"I'll call Miranda," I said finally. Mom kissed me and told me to have a good time. When I left for Miranda's house Mom was washing the breakfast dishes and humming the "Sesame Street" song. I never knew that dumb song could sound so good.

Miranda and I decided to walk from her house to the Pay 'n' Save drugstore. It's almost a mile, and Miranda hippity-hopped the whole way. She asked me a million questions about Erin even though I'd already told her everything over the phone.

She told me about Goofy escaping while she was in heat and how mad her mom had been when she caught Goofy with Abner, the meanest, ugliest three-legged dog you've ever seen. Miranda said I could have one of the puppies when they were born. No way would I ever want one, but I didn't tell her that.

At the Pay 'n' Save we bought matching neon pink note-books. We bought pens with four colors—pink, green, turquoise, and purple—and little plastic zipper cases to put them in. We bought pencils, Scotch tape, and notebook paper. Miranda got the wide-ruled kind. Her handwriting is so loopy she needs the extra space. I got college-ruled.

Miranda wondered if we should buy crayons, but I told her no way, not for seventh grade. We got colored pencils instead, for making maps in geography. When we were all done we started for home. Miranda talked without stopping.

Miranda loves to talk. She tells stories and jokes and makes faces when she talks. She's a lot of fun to listen to. She says things out loud that I think inside my head but never say. Sometimes it gets her in trouble, especially with her mom, but I like that about her. She's brave.

I like to talk too, just not as much. I think about what I want to say first, then I say it, as long as it's not too private. Miranda listens when I talk, but not as well as I listen to her. She's always thinking of what to say next. Sometimes she interrupts. I don't mind much. Nobody ever said friends are perfect. Anyway, that's the way it is most of the time.

While walking home that day from the Pay 'n' Save, Miranda chattered on and on about camp. She talked about falling out of her canoe, having to get up at six, putting a frog in her counselor's bed. When she was all finished talking about camp, she talked about school, what she would wear, how horrible all the homework would be, how awful it would be with no recess. She skipped ahead and told me to hurry up; then she asked me if I knew that Benji Tomazzi's big sister Marie had gotten pregnant.

I didn't hurry, and I didn't listen very well, not like I usually do. I felt like a balloon was blowing up inside me, growing bigger and bigger, getting fatter and tighter and ready to pop any second. I wanted to tell someone all the things I knew, the things about Dad, even if that someone was Miranda. I knew she wouldn't understand. How could she? I had to tell.

Miranda's head bobbed up and down ahead of me. The sun shone on her red hair, and it was as bright as a new penny. She was saying something about girls who get pregnant. I didn't hear her words, not really. There wasn't anyone else. There was only Miranda.

"My dad said he was going to kill himself." I didn't mean it to come out so loud, but it did. Miranda froze. She turned around in slow motion. Her mouth was still open from talking. She blinked her big eyes twice.

"*What did you say?*"

I took a deep breath.

"Remember when he was in the hospital?"

Miranda nodded. Her mouth was still open.

"He told Mom he wanted to kill himself."

"Did he try?" Miranda's voice was barely a whisper.

"No." I started walking.

Miranda caught up to me. "Is he okay now?"

"I don't know," I said. "He promised my mom to go back to the doctor. He's taking some medicine."

"Is that why he sleeps all the time? Is it from the medicine?" I wondered how Miranda knew about Dad sleeping all the time. We hadn't played at my house for a long time. I must have let it slip, given away clues. I felt my neck and face turn red.

"How should I know why he sleeps so much?" I snapped. I was embarrassed and wished I hadn't told. We walked for a couple of blocks without saying anything. Miranda kicked at a Pepsi can.

"That happened to my mom once," she said finally. "Sleeping all the time, I mean." I looked over at her but she didn't look back. She was watching the sidewalk pass beneath our feet. I waited for her to say more. She walked beside me without bouncing. She took a deep breath and started to talk. "Remember when I told you about Stacy?"

I nodded. Stacy was Miranda's little sister. She'd been killed in a car accident the year before the Evanciches moved to our neighborhood. Her picture was up on the mantel at Miranda's house. She'd been a cute little kid with freckles. Miranda didn't talk about her much.

"Well, after Stacy died Mom and Dad and Terry and I, we cried every day, every time we thought about her. I never knew people could cry so much, but we did. We all did. My dad cried most of all. Do you know what it's like to see your own dad cry?" I nodded but Miranda didn't see me. She stopped and wiped her nose on the sleeve of her T-shirt.

"After a while my mom stopped acting normal. She didn't go anywhere. She didn't brush her hair or put on her makeup. She didn't check under my fingernails for dirt or yell at me for burping or anything."

"What happened?" I asked.

"Dad took her to a doctor. He took her a couple of times a week. After a long time she got better."

I thought about beautiful Mrs. Evancich and tried to picture her with hollow, staring eyes. I imagined her curled up on the couch, sloppy and uncaring, half alive, skinny and pale and uninterested in her very own kids. It was hard to believe.

"I bet you guys miss Stacy sometimes," I said. Miranda nodded. I put my arm around her neck. I thought of my own tiny sister, how awful it would be if anything ever happened to her. Then I thought about Dad and wondered if he would ever be well enough to make elephant feet with Erin. The thought of it made me smile.

Mrs. Evancich got better. Dad would get better too. He *had* to. It's what Mom hoped. It's what I hoped too, more than anything in the whole world.

Miranda slipped her arm around my waist, and we walked together all the way home, thinking about our sisters and our families, not saying a word, just being close, just being best friends.

MIRANDA asked me to stay for lunch. She didn't say anything more about Stacy, and I didn't talk about my Dad. We had peanut-butter-and-jelly sandwiches and juice out of little boxes.

Miranda talked constantly, stopping only to take bites, drink, and breathe. She asked if I was going to buy hot lunches or take a sack lunch to school. After Dad lost his job, my teacher sent a note home saying I could get free hot lunch. I never did. Not even once. I told Miranda I would be taking my lunch.

"Me too," said Miranda. "Hot lunch is pure puke."

"*Miranda Elaine!*" yelled Mrs. Evancich from the kitchen.

"My mom has radar ears," said Miranda. She rolled her eyes and stuck out her tongue toward the kitchen. I laughed so hard juice almost came out of my nose.

When we were finished eating I told Miranda I had to get going. For once she didn't beg me to stay. "Call me next time you want to go to the fort," she said. "Let's try to go one more time before school starts." I said O.K. and hurried down the street toward home.

The first place I looked for Dad was on the couch. He wasn't there. Then I went into the kitchen to see if it looked like he'd eaten any lunch. There was a note propped up against the sugar bowl.

Trina,
   I went to visit Mom and Erin at the hospital. I'll come home with Mom at supper time. How about some BLTs? There's bacon in the fridge, and you can get tomatoes and lettuce from the garden. Love, Dad
P.S. Look on your pillow for a surprise.

I must have stared at that note for ten minutes. I couldn't remember the last time Dad had written me any kind of a note. It was just a little note, nothing special. I read it and read it. It was a totally normal note, a normal thing a dad would write. I should have been really happy to get that note, but it made me feel kind of funny instead, at least at first.

Dad hadn't done anything normal for a long time. For him, not normal was normal. Sleeping and not eating and not being interested in anything were normal, or at least that's what I was used to. So writing me a note wasn't really normal for him, even though it should have been. That's what made me feel funny. Dad was acting strange.

Could his medicine have worked that fast? It seemed impossible. But he'd told Mom he would take it. And now he was doing normal things for the first time in a long time. He'd gone to visit Mom! I could hardly believe it. And he'd left me a note. I kissed Dad's note and read it once more.

Look on your pillow for a surprise.

All of a sudden I was burning with curiosity. I ran upstairs three steps at a time. I flung open the door to my room and ran in. There on my pillow was one of my old Golden Book encyclopedias. I read those books a million times when I was little.

The encyclopedia was open to the page that explains eclipses. Stuck to the page was one of those sticky yellow notes. Dad had drawn an arrow pointing to the drawing of a lunar eclipse. "Tonight," he'd written. "Starts at 1:34."

I picked up the encyclopedia and hugged it. I read the note again and again. I knew exactly what the surprise was. Dad and I were going to watch an eclipse, just like before. The medicine *was* working.

The first time I saw an eclipse I was six years old. Dad woke me up and wrapped me in a sleeping bag. He carried me outside to where he'd set up a lawn chair by the barn. It must have been in the fall because I remember the smell of the leaves and the clouds my dad's breath made in the cold air. I sat in his lap and together we watched the moon as it slowly turned dark.

That night Dad sang all the songs he knew that had the word *moon* in them. He sang "Moonglow" and "Moon-shadow" and "Moon Over Miami" and "By the Light of the Silvery Moon." Then when he ran out of real moon songs he sang "Old MacDonald Had a Moon" and "Home, Home on the Moon" and "Row, Row, Row Your Moon." I laughed so hard I wished he would never stop.

That's the way my dad used to be, before all the bad things happened, before he changed. And now he was taking his medicine and wanted me to see the eclipse. He was going to get well. Everything was going to be just like it used to be.

I stuck the sticky note to the end of my nose. I hopped around and around, twirling and hugging myself and thinking about the eclipse. Then I saw myself in the long mirror, goofing around like that, and I thought of Miranda. I was acting just like her! It made me laugh. I laughed so hard I fell on my bed and rolled around. An eclipse with my dad! I could hardly wait. It was too too *too* good to be true.

The BLTs were waiting when Mom and Dad came home. Mom looked pale, but she smiled when I told her dinner was ready. Dad smiled at me too, for the first time in a long time, but his eyes were so sad that I wondered if his back was hurting extra that day. I hoped it didn't hurt too much to watch the eclipse.

Mom talked about Erin while we ate. She said the doctor thought Erin could come home in a few more days, that her weight was coming up and she was getting a lot stronger. She was even learning to eat without the special bottle.

"I nursed her twice today," said Mom. "She ate like a little pig!" Mom laughed and her blue eyes sparkled. It was great news. Soon our family would be together the way it should be.

Dad didn't say much, but at least he was eating with us. He ate two sandwiches and even a bowl of ice cream for dessert. When we were finished, he excused himself to go feed and milk Priscilla. Right before he went out the back door he turned around and said, "Don't forget about tonight, Trina," and then he was gone.

"What's that all about?" asked Mom. I told her about the eclipse. "He sure must be feeling better," she said. "I couldn't believe it when he showed up this morning to spend the day with me at the hospital."

"It's his medicine, Mom," I said. "He must be taking it again, just like he said he would."

Mom nodded. "I hope so, Trina," she said, and I wondered why she didn't sound as happy as I felt.

After supper I washed the dishes and cleaned up the kitchen. Mom and I watched TV for a while, but the show was stupid and it was hard for me to concentrate. All I could think about was the eclipse.

Mom went up to bed at nine. Dad still hadn't come in, but I figured he was probably working in the barn or in the garden. I decided to try to read something. I had four and a half hours to fill up.

I went up to my room and dug through my books looking for something good to read, something that would make the time go fast. I passed up *The Yearling*. Too sad. *Gone with the Wind*. Too thick. Nothing looked good. I looked through a pile of old magazines. Then I remembered my encyclopedias.

I started with the *A* book. I read from the back to the front, leafing through until I found pictures that caught my eye. I read about Assyria and Antarctica and Alabama. I read for an hour. Then I picked up the *M* book. After that I read the *C*. I tried to concentrate, but a bunch of times I realized I'd scanned a whole paragraph without thinking about what I'd read.

It was hot in my room. The upstairs is always hot at

night, even when it is cool outside. It was quiet except for the soft, whispery sound my curtains made as the breeze blew them in and out against the window.

I got tired of reading and flopped down on my bed. It was 12:27.

I woke up with a jerk and stared at the clock: 1:25. I couldn't believe I'd fallen asleep. I grabbed a sweatshirt in case it was cool outside. I slid into a pair of flip-flops and tiptoed downstairs. My heart was racing. I had the same feeling I used to get when I played hide-and-seek in the dark. The frog was dancing in my belly, but it was a good feeling for once, a good kind of nervous. I couldn't wait to find my dad.

DAD hadn't said where to meet, but I was sure it would be where we had watched the eclipse when I was six. I hurried down the pathway toward the barn. There aren't any big trees around the barn, so you can see more of the sky at once. I knew I'd find him there.

There was a full moon that night. Its silvery light made puddles on the ground between the shadows of the trees. I stepped in the light places, surprised by how much shadow I made, moon shadows, like in the song Dad had sung. I wondered if he'd sing tonight. The breeze ruffled the leaves in the trees. I was glad I'd thought of wearing a sweatshirt.

Dad was leaning against the corral fence. His head was bent and through the moonlight I could see the slump of his bony shoulders, the crooked curve of his back where he had hurt it. I coughed a couple of times so I wouldn't startle him. His head came up and he listened, but he didn't turn around.

I climbed up the fence next to where Dad was standing and sat on the top rail. For a while neither of us spoke. The moon above us was fat and round, the color of melted gold.

"Remember the last time we did this?" asked Dad. His voice was quiet and low.

"I remember." I looked up at the moon. The eclipse had

begun, and one fingernail clipping of the moon was now in shadow. "The eclipse took a long time."

"I held you the whole time."

"I was wrapped up in the sleeping bag," I said. "Did your arms get tired?"

"Do you know how long Mom and I had to wait until you came along?" asked Dad.

"Eighteen years," I said. Dad nodded and stared at the night sky.

"My arms never got tired." He reached for my hand and we watched the moon together. It was a little darker. Not much, but a little. I picked out Mars and Venus. Dad had taught me to find them when I was four. Dad's hand was big and rough. It felt good.

We watched for a long, long time without saying anything.

Now the moon was halfway in the shadow of the Earth. The shadowed part, the eclipsed part, was dark, rusty red. An owl hooted from one of the big trees.

"Do you remember all those moon songs?" I asked.

"You mean like 'Old MacDonald Had a Moon'?" I laughed. "That was a long time ago, Trina," said Dad.

"Six years isn't *that* long."

"Feels like a million years to me."

Chico snorted somewhere in the pasture. The shadow slid across the moon.

"Mom's going to need your help when the baby comes home," said Dad.

"We'll both help her," I said. "It won't be that bad."

"Sometimes things don't work out the way we plan." He turned to me and squeezed my hand. I didn't look at him. I could feel his eyes on me. I watched the moon. My heart started to beat fast and I wasn't sure why. I took a deep breath.

"I wish you didn't worry so much, Dad." I made my voice sound strong, grown-up. I wondered if Dad could hear my heart.

"I'm not worried," he said. "Not anymore." *The medicine,* I thought. *He must be taking it.*

"I'm glad you're taking your medicine again." I stared at the moon. It was mostly dark. I could feel Dad's eyes on me. It made me feel just a little squirmy. Maybe I shouldn't have mentioned his medicine. *Look at the moon,* I wanted to say. *That's what we came out here for.*

"I'm sorry for all the hurt I've caused you and Mom," said Dad. His voice was almost a whisper. He squeezed my hand so hard it hurt. Tears welled up in my eyes from nowhere. I wiped my eyes on my sweatshirt sleeve.

"It's okay, Dad," I said. "The same thing happened to Miranda's mom, but look at her now!" I tried to smile, but smiling is hard when your face is trying to cry. "Everything is okay now."

"Remember when we took that trip to the Oregon caves?" he asked. I nodded. I'd never forget that place; the damp coolness in the middle of summer, stalactites and stalagmites all over the place. "Remember when the guide turned all the lights out?"

"It was so dark we couldn't even see our own hands," I said.

"That's how it's been for me, Trina." Dad's voice was harsh and quivery. "Dark. So dark." It scared me, the sound of his voice. Dad started to cry. His bony shoulders shook as he sobbed. "I'm so sorry."

My own hot tears slid down my face in little rivers, dripping off my chin. I looked up at the moon. It was completely covered now and as red as blood. I leaned over and hugged my dad.

"But remember when it was all dark in the cave, Dad?" I made my voice sound bright and cheerful. "How the guide lit that one little match, and all of a sudden you could see everything again?"

It didn't seem like he heard me. I talked louder.

"Just one little match! Can you believe it? One little teeny light. It lit up the whole cave." How could I make him listen? "Just have a little hope, Dad, I mean, like that little match. Things are getting better. We're all here for you, me, Mom, and now Erin. *Please* Dad, please don't cry."

"I know it's hard for you to understand," said Dad. He shook his head back and forth, back and forth. He looked up at me and even in the dark I could see how bright his eyes were, how bright and sad and wild.

"But I *do too* understand," I cried. "I'm not some baby. Mom told me. She told me about your . . . sickness. Mrs. Evancich got better, Dad. She got better!"

Dad started petting my hair really hard. He squeezed me and cried and petted me. "Forgive me, Trina Jean."

My face was pressed up against his chest. I could smell his sweat and hear his pounding heart, the raspy sound of his sobbing. I wanted to tell him that I loved him too, but I couldn't get the words out. My own heart was racing and my mouth was dry.

"Why don't we go in now, Dad," I said. I used that same, calm voice Mom uses. I felt like I would smother. I had to get away. I felt Dad nod his head. He took a deep breath.

"You go on in," he whispered. He let me go. "I want to be by myself for a while longer."

"Are you okay?" I asked.

"Yeah, I'm fine."

I climbed down from the fence and took a couple of deep breaths. The night air had suddenly turned freezing cold. I shivered and walked toward the house.

"Never forget how much I love you," Dad called quietly.

"I won't," I said, and hurried into the house.

I undressed and put on my sleeping T-shirt. I tossed the encyclopedia on the floor beside my bed and climbed between the sheets. I squeezed my eyes shut tight, wishing I could fall asleep, wishing I could get the picture of my crying dad out of my brain. He'd never cried in front of me before. It made me feel sick thinking about it.

Never forget how much I love you. I remembered Dad's words and shivered, like a big spider was walking up my back. The way he'd said it just sounded so . . . *final.*

I jumped out of bed, flung open my door, and ran down the stairs. "Trina?" called Mom. "Is that you?"

I ran through the kitchen, knocking over a high chair with a crash. My hands were shaking as I fumbled with the doorknob. I pulled open the back door with a jerk, but the screen door was stuck. I hit it hard. Mom was behind me in the kitchen.

"What's wrong?" she asked.

"Dad!"

Boom! We both heard it. I kicked open the screen door and jumped off the porch.

"*No!* Trina!" she screamed.

I got as far as the barn and then stopped. I knew he was in there. Something inside me snapped. I started to scream. I screamed and screamed and screamed, the way Mr. Durkovic taught us to do if we ever thought someone was following us.

The porch light went on. The Abrigos' porch light went on. Mom came running out in her housecoat. Mr. Abrigo came running with all of his dogs barking.

I was bawling now, my throat hurt, and I was shaking so hard I could hardly stand up. I *had* to go in, but my legs wouldn't let me.

"Mitch!" screamed Mom. She ran into the barn, and I saw the darkness inside swallow her up. She switched on the light. Now I could see her back. I couldn't see Dad.

Mr. Abrigo shouted and ran into the barn.

I heard my own voice scream one last word.

"*Daddy!*"

I threw up, and then I fainted.

THE sirens woke me.

By the time Mrs. Abrigo helped me sit up an ambulance was flashing in our driveway and four medics were rushing toward the barn.

"Dad!" I cried, but my voice was barely a squawk. I was dizzy and confused. I remembered the shot. I started to cry hard. Mrs. Abrigo shushed me and rocked me like a baby. She was crying too.

Just then Mom came out of the barn. Mr. Abrigo had his arm around her and was helping her walk. She was sobbing, shaking so hard she could hardly take a step. One medic ran up to Mom and Mr. Abrigo. The other three ran into the barn. When they came out they had my Dad between them.

Alive!

Two of the medics helped Dad walk. He walked like his legs were rubber. A couple of times I thought he would fall. His hands covered his face. He moaned and shook and never looked up. They led him to the ambulance shaking and stumbling.

Alive!

I blubbered with happiness. Snot ran down my nose, but

I didn't care. The ambulance drove off with its lights flashing. Mom went in the ambulance with Dad.

The Abrigos took me inside. Mrs. Abrigo made me sit down. I felt weak and shaky, like I might throw up again any second. She got me a tissue and a glass of water. Mr. Abrigo sat across from me and held my hand. He told me it looked like Dad had changed his mind at the last second, how the gun had gone off but no one was hurt. Mr. Abrigo shook his head from side to side, and I thought he looked about a million years old. Mrs. Abrigo made us hot chocolate. By the time we were finished drinking it, the sun was coming up.

Mrs. Abrigo told me I had to go to bed. I told her no way could I ever sleep, not after all of that, but she insisted. She waited outside the bathroom door and reminded me to brush my teeth. She even tucked me in, like I was five years old. I must have fallen asleep right away, because the next time I looked at my clock it said nine o'clock. Mrs. Abrigo was asleep in the chair beside me.

Mom called right after that. She said Dad was in a special hospital, a mental hospital. He was all drugged up. She told me it would be better if he didn't have visitors for a few days. That was fine with me. I didn't feel ready to see him anyway.

Mom told me that she loved me. She asked me to send some of her clothes with Mr. Abrigo because she was still in her nightgown and robe. She sounded as rotten as I felt.

Mrs. Abrigo made breakfast. To me it tasted like rubber. At eleven, Mr. Abrigo left to pick up Mom and take her to Saint Teri's to take care of Erin. Mrs. Abrigo and I did dishes, and then I told her in my most grown-up voice that she should go home and rest.

"I can't leave you, Trina baby," she said. "Not after what happened. You shouldn't be alone."

"Mom said she'd be back around three," I said. "And I want to go back to bed." That must have sounded like a good idea to Mrs. Abrigo, because she smiled and nodded her head.

"That's just what you need, honey. Lotsa sleep will make you feel better." She agreed to go home and rest. I agreed to go back to bed, even though I knew I wouldn't be able to sleep. She left out the back door and said for me to call her if there was anything I needed. I said O.K. and waved good-bye. Then I went straight upstairs.

The upstairs was already stifling hot. My legs and arms felt like heavy wood. My eyes hurt and my head pounded. I passed the door to my room and went down the hall to Mom and Dad's room. The curtains were still shut. The bed was a mess. It was dark and still and I had to lie down.

I fell onto Mom's side of the bed. The pillow smelled like her. I buried my face in it and breathed until all I could smell was Mom. I wished she were there. I needed her to hold me.

I reached for the phone and dialed Miranda's number.

"Hello?"

"It's me, Trina."

"We heard," said Miranda. "About your dad. It's just *horrible.*"

"Who told you?"

"Father Tom called really early. He said we should all say a prayer for your dad. He called everyone from church." Tears made it hard for me to see.

"Can you come over?" I asked. I felt like a pair of hands were squeezing my throat.

"Here I come right now," said Miranda, and slammed down the phone.

Five minutes later I heard the back door open and shut. "Trina?" called Miranda.

"Up here!"

Miranda ran up the stairs and into the room. She dived into the bed beside me. For once she didn't say a word.

I told her everything. I told her about the eclipse, how I thought Dad was getting better, how excited I'd been to meet him. I told her about him crying, about how he'd squeezed me so hard I thought I'd smother, how he'd told me he loved me, how I'd wanted to tell him that I loved him too.

My breath came fast and hard, my throat tightened, until I thought I would choke to death, but I kept talking. I told Miranda about hearing the shot, about screaming, about throwing up and fainting. About Dad, alive, walking out of the barn between the two medics. Miranda put her arms around me.

I cried hard and long, longer than I've ever cried. I screamed and bawled, until I thought my throat must be bleeding inside. My nose felt like a baseball. I could hardly open my eyes. I tried to stop sniffling but I couldn't. My sobs were like big spasms, shaking me and making me sob even more. Miranda held me tight.

After a while she reached over and handed me a tissue from the box next to the bed. She took one for herself. Her eyes were red too. She whispered in my ear, "My dad says the more you cry, the less you have to pee." She looked into my eyes and smiled. I smiled back.

We blew our noses at the exact same time, and it sounded like a big honk. I saw Miranda bite her lower lip. A grin curled the ends of her mouth. We blew our noses again. I think I giggled first.

Pretty soon we were both giggling and honking and rolling on the bed.

"I guess I'll never pee again," I said, and we laughed even harder.

When we were done I felt like I could sleep for a year. All of my horrible feelings were gone. Miranda lay on her side and faced me. Our noses were almost touching.

"He's alive, Trina. Don't forget."

"I won't."

Miranda was right. Dad was alive because he'd changed his mind. And if he was alive he could get better. For the first time I felt a little real hope, like that match in the dark, dark cave.

I reached for Miranda and she wrapped her long arms around me. We hugged for a long time, not saying anything. Then suddenly Miranda pushed me away.

"Hey, look," she said. She pulled her T-shirt tight across her chest. There, right where they should be, were two little bumps. "I wanted you to be the first to see." I grinned so hard my face hurt.

IN the past three days I've cried a lot. I cried with Mom when she came home from the hospital that first night. We talked about Dad, about how scared we both had felt. Mom told me how Erin hadn't gained any more weight. She cried so hard about Erin that the front of her T-shirt got soaked from her milk. We're still waiting for Erin to come home.

I cried when I woke up the next night with nightmares about guns and screaming and my dad lying dead with his head blown off. I got into bed with Mom. When I told her the dream she cried too.

I cried when the doctor called on Saturday to say Dad was asking for us, that he was responding well to his medicine, that we should be able to see him in a few days. I cried later that day when Mr. Abrigo came over to tell Mom not to worry about money, that he had a little something that was just wasting away in the bank.

I cried in church yesterday when Father Tom had everyone say a silent prayer for our family. The tears trickled down my cheeks and my nose ran, until Miranda elbowed me and I peeked through my tears to see her pull a new white bra strap from the neck of her dress and give it a snap.

Mrs. Evancich poked her. I had to bite my cheek so I wouldn't giggle.

That was yesterday, Sunday. Today is Monday, and now I'm a seventh grader, sitting in a beat-up old desk in Room 5, Mrs. Renchek's class. Miranda's in art class right now. I wonder what she's doing. We walked to school together this morning. Right before math we talked for a while, but Mr. Meyers made us sit in alphabetical order, so we were way across the room from each other. She said to meet her after school. It'll be fun to hear all about her classes.

Dad's doctor says we can go visit him tomorrow. He said Dad's going to be in the hospital for a long time, probably more than a month, but we'll be able to see him. Mr. Abrigo said he'd drive us tomorrow after school. I'm nervous. And a little scared. Part of me doesn't want to see him at all, but I have to anyway. Dad needs me. We need each other. If I think about it too much I'll start to cry again. I cried a lot last summer. That's what I could never write in an English paper. I almost lost my dad and got a new sister named Erin. Now that I'm a big sister, I feel older. That's another thing that happened last summer. I stopped feeling like such a little kid.

A fat boy just went up to Mrs. Renchek's desk. She's looking at him over the top of her glasses. He must have asked her to go to his locker or something. She's shaking her head no and her jiggly neck is flapping. I haven't laughed once. I think I'm going to like Mrs. Pelican. She has nice eyes.

Someone just knocked at the door. "Come in," says Mrs.

Renchek, and we all turn to look. A big girl walks in. She looks almost like a grown-up woman. She's wearing panty-hose. She must be in ninth grade. She's taking a note to Mrs. Renchek. Mrs. Rencheck is reading it. Now she's getting up and walking down our row.

"This is for you, Trina," she says, and hands me the note. It's on pink paper.

Wait for Mr. A. on the front steps after school. We're going to pick up Erin! Love, Mom

Everyone is staring at me, but I don't care. If Miranda were here I'd dance around the class with her and hop and laugh and yell! I'll tell her when I see her after school. She won't mind walking home alone, not this time.

There are only five more minutes until the bell rings, and I'm not finished with my composition. I forgot a couple of details.

What I Did Last Summer

by Trina Stenkawsky   English Rm. 5

Last summer I rode my horse a lot. His name is Chico and he's a gelding, not a stallion. That means he can't have children. My friend Miranda Evancich and I made a fort down in the gulch on the other side of the train tracks. Whenever we go there we race. Miranda's horse is named Tonka. Chico and Tonka have matching bridles. They were a present from Miranda's mom.

Chico is faster than Tonka, but Miranda keeps saying that Tonka should beat Chico because his legs are longer. Once I hit my knee really bad against a tree when we were racing, but it was only a bruise.

Miranda has this dog named Goofy. Goofy is an Airedale terrier, and if she doesn't get enough exercise, she jumps on everyone. All last summer Miranda brought Goofy on our rides. Afterward we would spend about an hour pulling burrs and stickers out of her fur. Once when Miranda was mad at me, she said my hair was just like Goofy's. Boring, brown, and fuzzy. At least my hair isn't <u>carrot orange</u> like hers.

Last summer I helped my mom with day care when my dad was in the hospital. He was sick. Mom paid me five dollars a week to help. I made lunch and Kool-Aid and watched the kids from nine to eleven in the morning so Mom could go to see a friend. There were four kids.

Wayne is five and he cries and fusses a lot. I call him Whine but not in front of his mom. Marissa is Wayne's little sister and she is two. She gets lots of ear infections and takes pink medicine, which she spits out. It's a pretty color, the medicine, I mean, but I don't like it all over my clothes.

Glendon is three years old. He has the biggest eyes, black like coal, my mom says. Glendon's mom had a baby last spring. The baby's name is Trinidad. It means Trinity in Spanish. Trinity is the Father, Son, and Holy Ghost. Trinidad started coming to day care right after school was out. He is the color of caramel (my favorite candy) and is fat and soft. He smiles a lot.

I don't miss the day-care kids, except for Trinidad and maybe Glendon a little, because I like how he said my name Tweena. My mom had a baby two weeks ago. So she can't do day care for a while. ~~Our baby is still at the hospital. My dad is at a hospital too, but it's a different one. Before he went to the hospital, we watched an eclipse of the moon. It's pretty quiet at our house right now. THE END~~ My new sister's name is Erin Elaine. She is beautiful, a <u>million</u> times cuter than Trinidad, and she has red hair, just like I did when I was born. We are bringing her home <u>today</u>!!!

Tomorrow we are going to visit my dad. He is in the hospital again, but it's a different hospital from before, a better one. The doctor says Dad has a good chance of getting well, but it might take a while. I bet we will take Erin when we go. Won't Dad be surprised to see her!

This summer, Dad and I watched an eclipse, like we did when I was six. For a minute the moon was completely dark, but I've seen an eclipse before, and I knew it wouldn't last forever. Eclipses never do.

THE END